Th

MW00459932

the sequel to The Coming

By Tyler G. Johnson

"I do not think that all who choose wrong roads perish; but their rescue consists in being put back on the right road."

-Clive Staples Lewis
The Great Divorce

"Do not be too eager to deal out death in judgment. Even the very wise cannot see all ends."

-J.R.R. Tolkien,
The Fellowship of The Ring

One

.

I had stepped through a membrane that was suspended in the air and entered. We had effortlessly broken through to the other side. The best way I can describe that moment is by saying that it suddenly felt like for my whole life on earth there had been unseen hands clenched about my neck, choking me of air and keeping me from truly breathing, but the instant we came through and into this place they had simply fallen off. I could take large, slow breaths. My mind was exceedingly clear. All of the pain (both physically and emotionally) that I had grown familiar with, so familiar that I had even become accustomed to it and forgotten about it, abruptly melted out of my being and thus reminding me of its reality all of this time. Peace is an understatement; absolute serenity was unavoidable. It ambushed you without consent. These are a fraction of the things I experienced when I merely breathed the air of this place, what I later learned is referred to by its inhabitants as "The Abode".

And though it is only a lower level, it still contains things and sights and concepts that would be utterly impossible for your mind to conceive or understand. For this reason I won't describe the greatest of wonders in this place for they would make no sense to you; you would completely miss their intrinsic value, thus negating any reason for me to share about them with you.

It would be like trying to communicate to an Eskimo (wbo has been forced into celibacy through mere seclusion) the joy of walking a Hawaiian beach at sunset with your spouse. He has known nothing but snow and cold and loneliness; the thought of warm waters and sand, breaching whales that are to look at rather than kill, being outside with few clothes on, and the absolute feeling of *home* when you touch your spouse's skin would be total foreignness to him. He would likely ask how and why those things are good, because one has no concept of value for things that exist outside of their world and understanding, and wearing few clothes and not taking the kill when spotting a whale would not sound like wisdom to him, but folly and death. His world is wholly different from the sands of Wailea, and he has no reason to desire them. This, as it turns out, is also the the same line of reasoning why many choose to stay in the regions below ours rather than come breath the air here, but we will traverse those paths later on in this story.

The reason your mind would not be able to understand some of the things in this place is because the same laws that govern your world are not the same that govern this world. There is a degree of learning everything all over again, and those that enter this place with the heart of a child start off better than those that think they know how things work. Some come here and simply have fun as they learn, like the toddler that is learning to negotiate defying gravity by attempting to walk. Some laugh as they learn and stumble and learn again, but some are simply befuddled by these new realities, and it not coincidence that it is usually those that think they know how things work that also find themselves perplexed. Let me be clear; you will know very little how this world works, for it is under a government very different from what you have known in the past. This, be assured, is part of the joy of this place. It isn't just a new realm of earth; it is a whole new world to be explored and known.

And that is exactly what I did for a very long time. What I found in those years, or what I would assume were years, were beyond the dreams of all men joined together. Just ten steps into the unexplored regions and all ability to fathom beauty is torn down, vanquished, and rebuilt. Every subsequent step it is remodeled again and again. I have never felt so unlearned, weak, and humbled, all I may add, now caused me jocundity with no humiliation in the mix.

On these walks I learned at such a rate that one step forward could only be paralleled to a lifetime of study and experience in my past life. The changes within me were so dramatic that I became a new creation over and over again with each passing moment. The "me" that was but a moment ago was so different from who I was at the next instant that I couldn't see enough similarities between the two to call them both "me"; I had already been made new. I must remind you that this was simply by *looking* at my surroundings on a mere walk into the outlying regions outside where The City was located. Just the simple glance of the grass underfoot would cause extreme inebriation.

It was the greatest delight of delights to learn how small I was, for it only pointed to how great The Eternal desired me to be; He had always positioned us as the pinnacle of creation, so if the created order around me possessed such greatness, surely He was making me even greater in beauty, wisdom, creative expression, and patience.

I went as far as I could into these regions, like an extension of Lewis and Clark, only these lands stretch further than anyone could ever travel for all of the time encompassed in eternity. Just as time in this place, the lands here are never-ending. One can go and never come back, for there is no limit or final boundaries to their boarders. And I suppose one would be completely euphoric in that undertaking alone, without company, home, or banqueting tables. But nobody would do that, for this world is about one thing and one thing only; seeking pleasure. Our commission is and always was hedonistic in nature. This is why it was rare for one to explore very far. For though beauty and fulfillment can be found in one blade of grass underfoot, the greatest of pleasure still came from Joshua. Nobody wanted to be too far from Him, and He could usually be found in The City. When He did take a trip to the more wild territories of The Abode, many would go with Him. We had learned that while this whole world was heavenly, it was He that was heaven itself.

As I stated before, when Joshua and I first arrived we initially went to The City. That is the brief version. In actuality, after we came through that membrane and into this world we walked for quite some time until we were but a few hundred yards from The City.

It was a monstrosity of a city, too glorious to describe semantically in a way that would do it complete justice. It glowed like the sun and towered above us, its height communicating that it been there for millions of years, far before my existence.

Joshua motioned to me with his hand and we continued walking towards the city. As we got closer, Joshua looked down at the ground and pointed to a long line that was deeply etched in the terrain, like a scar on this world's skin.

"There used to be a wall here, with pearl gates at certain places. But walls and gates are meant to keep some out and others in. There is no need for that now. Who would we keep out and who would we keep in?"

Joshua smiled at me like He had a secret, stepped over the small ditch leftover from what I assumed was the removal of the wall and gates, and we made our way into the city.

Two

There were multitudes waiting for our arrival, lining the streets and making a corridor of bodies that decided for us where to walk. The cheering started the moment we rounded the corner and was deafening but not unenjoyable. I felt very important walking down this passageway with Joshua, having so much attention lavished in my direction, but I was reminded that they were there solely for Joshua and His success in his second trip to the lowers lands, not really because I was there.

Joshua turned towards me, a smirk on His face, and gently said, "Oh, I disagree. It isn't that simple."

"What isn't that simple?"

"They aren't just celebrating Me, but you as well."

I had forgotten that He could read my insides without my mentioning of them.

"What are they celebrating me for?" I asked.

"Whether they are cheering for me or you makes no difference; I am woven through and into every good thing, and when something other than Me is praised here it is still Me who receives the praise. Here it is an obvious fact that I am to credit for everything, and that leads us to the freedom to praise one another. There is no more puffing up or false humility. With time you will learn how to receive this kind of honor. After all, it is not in the rejection of honor that men are most humbled but when they receive it knowing they don't deserve it.

You need to understand that they have been waiting for you, watching and witnessing your every move since you were birthed in the old world. Their story and what they did while in the lower lands had a direct influence upon you, and you had a direct influence on how their story worked out. They are proud of you. You are a part of how their actions on earth unfolded, and thus, their reward. You have made others rich without ever knowing it."

I looked at the faces that I was passing and noticed that while many's eyes were locked onto Joshua, some were surprisingly filled with tears and looking at me. I was struck with the reality that though I knew none here, there were many that already knew me fully. In this place that I felt as a stranger upon entrance I was in fact more at home, known, and understood than I could have ever been previously. There was no need for the pleasantries of introductions, at least on my part; they already knew of me.

We made our way along the street, a walkway composed of a metallic substance that was nearly transparent, but in no way not alive like the metals I had seen on earth. It wasn't long before I realized that this metal was gold, but not dead gold like the kind buried in the crust of the earth like I had seen. This gold was of such quality that the impurities, of which I now know caused much of the yellow color in the lifeless gold, were nonexistent, leaving it more like glass than the different hues that metals carried that I had known prior. Everything here, somehow, was transparent and opaque at the same time. You could see right through a thing and see it for what it was or stare at its outsides and see how it wanted to be seen. Everything was unveiled and veiled in fullness and at the same time; naked and clothed, private and public, yet always somehow without losing vulnerability and appropriateness. It was a realm of complete truth.

I suppose I should have had my gaze fixed on the beauty of those lining the streets or the architecture climbing to such great heights above me or Joshua Himself (the correct response, no doubt), but because of my infantile state at that time I was wholly transfixed on the mere ground. That is what it is like there; the thing of least importance in that world can capture your thoughts and heart far longer and deeper than the most glorious thing in the old world ever could.

The living corridor led us down different streets to a large building of sorts, one with wood doors that stood hundreds of feet tall. A dozen of the strongest men would have never been able to open these doors due to their weight, but as we drew near they opened slowly, inviting us in.

Joshua turned to me as we came through the doorway. "A banquet has been thrown in our honor. Let us feast."

Even in that entry room there was unspeakable beauties, but the first thing that ambushed me was the smell from the food that had been prepared for us. I had no idea fragrances could have such an effect upon a person. The smells cascading in from the dining room were so thick and manifest that they acted more as an appetizer than anything else. When one took in a breath through their nose, the aroma would quickly make its way through the nasal cavities to the tongue and bed down there, forming into actual tastes and textures in one's mouth. It was the oddest of sensations, since I had only known taste through the use of my mouth. This way of "smell" lured me to eat far more than smell had ever before. I was immediately unfed and ravenous. I later learned that in this place hunger is only a reality when it can be satisfied. Outside of that context it is completely absent.

The entry room that we were walking through was lined along the walls with men and women dressed in lavished attire that could be nothing less than the clothes of royalty.

Joshua whispered, "These are the kings and queens of earth. Some were royalty of the sort that sat on thrones, while others are of the royalty more lasting; the kind that served others in quietness and joy without a shred of honor. Many single mothers and widows line these walls. Bow, my friend. They deserve our honor."

And so we bowed to each that we passed. It made our travel to the dining room a slow process, and I have to admit that I wanted to get there in a hurry due to the holy seduction of smell hanging in the air. Yet the look that came from the eyes of each that we bowed to and bowed to us shifted something inside of me; after every brief interaction I felt stronger yet more aware of my weaknesses and thus humbled; a characteristic that every person of true royalty possesses and can impart, which each did to me.

Joshua bowed low. A few times on the upwards swing of his bow he would reach up and cup his hands on their cheeks, kissing them gently on the forehead or pause to smile at them. He lingered with each, in no rush to get anywhere or to do anything. I would assume that He made each person feel as though there was nothing else He had on His agenda but them, though He was only with each for a brief moment. That is the way it feels when one is with a real shepherd.

Food of that world is not like the food of the old world, as you may have guessed. Not only had the greatest cooks of all time been discipled in the arts of culinary by those that created the concept of food to begin with, but there were foods there that could not survive in the old world because of its leaning towards infection, rot, and wilt. Things that would have spoiled in moments there were wholly intact forever here, at least until someone ate them. Thus, the menu was completely different. Joshua sat next to me and I couldn't help but interrupt the conversation over and over simply to ask what it was that we were eating now, and now, and now, because I didn't want to miss out on not having it again due to the limitless dishes that were available. One could eat something and never have it again, not because it wasn't available or forgotten about but because there was so much more to try. You could have eaten a new thing every meal for the rest of eternity and would have never exhausted the menu.

It was a wonderful meal. Not only did we gorge upon food that was extravagant and delicious, but everyone in that banqueting hall, miles long as it is, could talk to one another at one time, somehow without talking over each other. I could hold a conversation with thirty people all at different places at the table without any trouble in the least. It wasn't that we were using our minds to speak to one another, but that our spirits didn't necessarily need our minds or our mouths to attain the goal of laughter or communication or even sight. I looked at all, spoke to all, and enjoyed all, all at the same time. This, as you can imagine, caused me a sense of utmost euphoria due to the connection I was having with so many wonderful people at the same time. All loved each other, all understood and valued each other, all interacted. The fellowship that one has here is exceptional and incomparable.

Some faces were familiar. This familiarity isn't referring to the effortless connection that one felt instantly upon engaging another person, but rooted in a life lived prior, in the old lands. One such face was my dear friend Rachel. It took a bit of time before I noticed her seated not far from me at the table. When I saw her I felt a range of emotions, not because I wasn't excited that she was there, but because I didn't understand *how* she got there. I was somewhat confused. The last time I had spoke with her, she was convinced that Joshua wasn't a paragon of virtue but a deceived and deceitful heretic. And if there was one thing that I had come to understand in this new place (I say "new" not because it is new at all, in fact it is very old, but because it is new to me) it was that nobody gets here without being escorted to it by Joshua. I got the sense that one can't make it here on their own for the path is too hard to traverse. One wouldn't know the way without Him showing it to them, and anyone (despite their intellectual predisposition) would be lost on their journey to this place if they went about on their own. This is why Rachel's presence caught me by surprise. Deduction led to me the assumption that she either was the first to make it here without the imperative of being escorted by Joshua, which I doubted (I could never even retrace my steps as to the path that led here and then find my way back again, it would be impossible), or she had changed her mind about Joshua.

"Rachel! You are here. I am so glad."

"Scythe, it is wonderful to see you."

She stood, walked over to me, and hugged me from behind as I was seated in my chair. I would have gotten up to greet her but she made her way over to me faster than I could react.

She stayed there clenching me for longer than one would normally, the way someone does when they are trying to communicate more than the simple "hello" that people do through normal hugs. It took some time, but after long enough I noticed that her body was gently and silently lurching here and there against my back. I held her head with my hands awkwardly over my shoulder, with her arms still wrapped tightly around me disallowing me to stand and properly greet her.

After long enough I forcefully unwrapped her arms from my chest and stood, turned around and embraced her. I could now see that I had guessed rightly; she was crying. Our last interaction had been one wrought with division, leaving us on different sides of an invisible line that was drawn in the sand.

"No need to feel guilty, Rachel. Everything is fine now." I said.

"Oh I couldn't feel guilt here if I wanted to. I am not weeping because of what I did, though it was rotten, but because of how you dealt with it. I am so proud of you. We can still feel here, though we never have reason to feel anything but joy. He only wiped away the tears that flow from pain. Tears of joy still flow like mountain streams. I am not sad; just glad to be united with you again."

I held her tight, like a brother does with a sister that he hasn't seen for years because they were both away at college. It felt good to be with her, like I had gained back a familiar part of me that had been missing.

My questions still needed to be answered. "But how? How are you here? The last we talked you wanted nothing to do with Joshua."

"That is why I am so proud of you. You didn't just guard your heart from bitterness when the Chosen rejected you, including me, but you continued to do what was right when nobody stood with you. You chose Him when nobody was. You led the way for the rest of us."

"What do you mean I led the way?"

"A few of us watched how you dealt with our rejection of you. Wisdom always leaves a backdoor to the possibility of being incorrect, especially when relationships are on the line over an issue. I have learned that one way to discern who is in the right and who is in the wrong in a situation is by stepping outside of the actual issue and argument at hand and just by watching the two parties interact with one another. Usually, the party that is in the right will carry themselves graciously and without offense when attacked, while the party that is in the wrong will make personal attacks and will carry themselves in a way that is dishonorable. I watched you respond peacefully when the Seers took everything from you. That spoke volumes to me. I knew that if your character was of such quality that you could be so gracious in your response after all that we did to you, that there was something to your claims. So, not long after you were asked to leave the Chosen, I made up my mind to find out more about Joshua."

At this moment, Joshua turned from his food and smiled at me, like he knew all along.

"You knew? And you didn't tell me?" I said.

"Yes I did. I didn't want to tell you something that would have caused you more joy coming from Rachel herself. After all, there was mending needed that only she could bring you, because it was a wound that happened between the two of you."

"Forgive me for my part of what happened, Scythe." Rachel said.

"Of course, Rachel. Without hesitation. I love you and am so glad you are here. When you went to find out more about Joshua, what happened?"

"I left in the direction I saw you walk in when you left. After some time I came upon a town, a town that I now know was the dwelling place of The Embrace. Everyone was gathered in a field, and I joined them to listen to Joshua. He only a said a few things, was distracted by a sickly looking fellow, then He started taking people with Him to this place. I don't know how it happened, but I went with Him. I didn't think that I qualified. I hadn't even gotten to talk to Him. My heart chose Him before my mind realized I had. But He saw my heart, so I was swooped up. Next thing I knew I was here. It felt like home, so I knew I had made the right choice, if the word "choice" is even the right word."

"You have never talked to Him?" I said.

"No, not officially." She said.

"Then let me introduce you. Rachel, meet Joshua."

Rachel knelt down on one knee, like a warrior does before a king prior to their promotion to knight. Joshua dabbed his mouth with his napkin, laid it on his plate, scooted his chair away from the table, then stood and looked down at Rachel for a brief moment before He dropped to His knees before her. There, at eye level, He embraced her.

I imagine the closest thing that can describe what it is like when He holds you (and not just for the first time) is much like the way a child must feel the first time they find a parent that they somehow lost years before, or a spouse that is reunited with the love of their life after years of thinking they had lost them to death. This person has learned how to provide for themselves, how to wrap themselves up so that they are warm at night, every moment remembering in grief what it was like when they were cared for and loved. Joshua's embrace feels like the day that nightmare is over because the impossible happens; the person suddenly finds their parent or spouse and is reunited with them. This is a fraction of the way your heart feels when He holds you. Everything outside of Joshua feels empty and cold and terrifying, but there, in His arms, you feel *found*.

After a few moments Joshua released her, and they both stood. Rachel was wiping her eyes, attempting to dry them. It was a bit too emotional of a moment for me so in hopes of shifting the mood I said,

"Well technically, you still haven't talked to Him."

Joshua and Rachel laughed, and Joshua stuck out His hand to her like he was a stranger and said, "Nice to meet you, maim." They shook hands and Rachel introduced herself sarcastically like it was the first time they had met. We all laughed, then Rachel waved to us and made her way back to her seat, still wiping her eyes.

Three

"What is he doing here?" I thought to myself, forgetting that all thoughts here are not held captive to privacy as they were before.

"Ah. Why do you ask?" Joshua replied, like I had asked out loud.

I wasn't sure why I had asked, so I just stayed quiet. I think more than anything I was just surprised that one of the Unenlightened was sitting at this table feasting alongside us, especially this specific man. He had been the forerunner of quite an awful event in the old lands during one of the times of adoration of the Chosen. I remembered him plainly because he was the only one that didn't wear a mask and didn't flinch when a young boy was gunned down while dancing on a stage.

Joshua's voice interrupted my thought. "I think I know why you thought that. And I think that maybe the two of you need to talk. It says if *you* have ought, then *you* initiate." Joshua said.

"Yes, but it also says 'ought with a brother'. Are you saying he is my brother?"

"Who isn't? When is someone not your brother or sister?"

"When they don't know You."

"Not exactly. I am not exclusive nor so rigorous in requirements towards family members. I am more inclusive than you realize. Family is family, despite what they do. All are children of the Eternal. A child is still someone's child even if they have never met the parent that brought them into this world."

"Are you saying that he got here without you helping him?" I said.

"No, not at all. Though all are children of the Eternal, they are free to live in His house or go about living somewhere else, foraging about in the garbage for what they need on their own like an orphan. Our job has always been to see them as family before they come into His house; to see them for who they will be when they live under His roof and act as the royalty they are destined to be. This is the foresight someone had with this man that used to be without enlightenment. Go talk to him to hear his story. It may help you understand."

While there isn't evil in the higher plains, that doesn't mean that some things don't still need to be refined and made perfect. We don't arrive here completed in the least bit. In fact, we arrive here much like we did in the lower lands; dependent, needy, and learning. We are always growing inside. To think otherwise would be to insult the Eternal's character; it would be to assume that one could discover all of Him with enough time. This is misinformed. We will continue learning and growing forever, becoming more and more like Him for the billions of millennia that spread before us.

I still needed much work. Joshua knew that part of that work would take place as things were made right between myself and others. The difference between this realm and the old isn't that we don't have to pursue reconciliation (things here are far more horizontal than many assume), but that when we pursue reconciliation it always takes place smoothly and fully. When something is needed to be made right, it is.

So I stood from the table once again, and walked over to the man.

"Uh, hello." I said awkwardly, not knowing the correct social protocol one should wield in greeting a killer.

"It's Scythe, right?" The man stood to greet me.

"Yes. And your name?" I replied dryly, a bit bored with the conversation already. If I could have wove a shrug into my response I would have. I had to remind myself that it was in my own interests to pursue this conversation or Joshua wouldn't have ever told me to do so.

"Lamia. But that was before. I'm not sure what I am to be called now. Sometimes Joshua renames us, but other times there is something salvageable in the name we had so He has us keep it. He hasn't told me yet what He has decided to do."

He seemed like the type who when asked a simple question that could be replied to sufficiently enough with one select word, would blabber on about something that vaguely related to the question asked in the first place until the listener wanted to turn and run in order to preserve their sanity. I didn't hate this man per say, at least not *yet*. I just didn't like him.

I steered the conversation in a new direction, hoping it would peak my interest more than the conversation had thus far. "So how did you get here, Lamia?"

"With Joshua, of course."

"Yes, I know that bit, but why? Or rather, how? You seemed quite pleased with your lifestyle when I saw you, taking delight in murder and all. What I can't work out isn't so much how you got *here*, but how you got to

Joshua to begin with. You didn't seem to have any desire for Him the last I saw you."

"I suppose I got to Joshua the same way you did."

"I went out of my way to find Him. You didn't."

Lamia frowned in disapproval. "No you didn't. He found you."

"That is true, at least to some degree. But..."

"No. He found you. Fully. You did nothing really." Lamia interrupted, speaking frankly.

"Well, I made decisions along the way to choose Him as well though." I said.

"I understand what you are saying. But even those choices were coxed along by His gentle nudges in the right direction."

He was right. I knew myself. Without Joshua's help every step of the way I would have fallen on the wayside as bitter, offended, and with only a facade of love rather the real thing. I was ruined without Him. And I was only aware of the efforts He made that I could see. I had a hunch there were countless times He worked on my behalf that I was totally blind to. To take any credit for my actions pertaining to doing the correct thing back in the lower regions was vain.

"So He found you too?" I asked.

"Yes. With much grace. You and I were both pursued and sought out, but we had two very different experiences. The 'how' is the same; but the 'where' is vastly different."

"Yeah?" I asked curiously, my interest finally captured.

"Well, that takes some explaining, and some of this Joshua wants to explain Himself. What I can tell you starts with that fateful day in the woods. Do you remember?"

"Yes." My mind flashed back to the songs of adoration rising up from the forest, the crashing of trees and brush as the vehicles and tanks rolled in, and Lamia standing before the crowd telling us that we must be punished for our crimes.

"After we murdered some of the people with you, I rounded up a few of the most beautiful women so that they could serve me back at the headquarters."

He paused as though he was thinking about something wholly different than what he was talking about.

"What is it?" I asked.

"Its so odd. I speak about those things without any shame. I am not proud of those things obviously, but I feel no grief over what I did. In fact, it doesn't feel like I ever did those things at all, though I know I did."

"Yes, I have noticed the same thing about this place." I said. "It is like guilt and shame are unable to enter one's heart when walking these streets and sitting at this table."

"Exactly. Sorry. Where were we? Let me see, ah yes, the women. You see, some of the other Unenlightened thought that I wasn't being just in the amount of women I was taking to be mine. I had just bound the women and put them in the vehicle when a few of them cornered me. It was the fruition of a mutiny that had been stirring for quite some time due to my torture of a few of my soldiers's spouses in hopes that I could gather information about a turncoat within our ranks. Turns out there never was one, by the way. Anyways, I gave a good fight but soon I took a baton hit to the cheek. That put me out. I woke up tied up, with my head under the vehicle, pressed up against one of the knobby off-road tires. Kneeled down on the ground on the opposite side of the vehicle from myself was one of the young men whose wife I had interrogated. He mumbled something about "true justice", got into the truck, and I heard the engine growl to life. I remember hearing him put it into gear and then incredible pressure on my skull. Next it was lights out. See, your experience with Joshua and being pursued by Him took place wholly on earth. Mine did not." Lamia said.

I thought for a moment. "But if His pursuit of your affections didn't take place on earth, where else could it have taken place?"

"Exactly." He said, supposing I already knew the answer, which I didn't fully, though I suppose I had an idea; an idea I couldn't fully admit to myself or even be totally conscious of because I had always been taught, and believed, something much different.

He went on. "Much grace was needed in my case. It is as you suspect. He found me in the world below."

Joshua suddenly hugged Lamia from behind. He had been standing there for a few moments before He did but I was so transfixed on what Lamia was saying that I didn't notice He was there.

"Thank you Lamia. That was perfect. I will explain more to Scythe later."

Lamia bowed to Joshua and sat back down in his seat to resume eating.

"Wow. You have some explaining to do." I joked.

Joshua laughed. "Yes, I suppose so. Grace has always needed a lot of explaining, at least for those not in the torrent of it at that particular moment, though I am not sure why. The only ones that don't ask questions are those whom are being lavished with it."

"Is that what this is about then? Grace?"

"Everything I do is about grace. You know that."

"I just didn't think grace was something we would, well, need *here.*"

"Why? Because everything is perfect here? So there is no need for grace because grace cannot exist with out there first being an infraction?"

"Yes, that is completely why."

"Things may be perfect here but there is still much to be made right. And the only way to restore something is through grace." Joshua said.

"Alright then. Teach me what needs to be restored."

"I will. I have something to show you. Come."

Four

One moment Joshua and I were in the banqueting hall, the next we were somewhere else. The relocation was so natural and undisturbing that it took place without notice in the course of blinking. I had my eyes open and looking at Joshua inside the hall, and when my eyes opened from the routine and nearly instantaneous sweep of my eyelids over my eyes, I found myself in a wholly new place altogether.

We were outside. The air was still as blissful as it was before, but something was odd about this place. It felt as though we were still on the same plane of reality that we had been, and it wasn't *bad* necessarily, for I am not sure that anything bad could survive in this world. But it did feel empty to some degree. We were standing in the middle of a street, surrounded on all sides by large mansions. Not far off in the distance I could see The City, with buildings in a steady stream between it and us.

"Where are we? I said.

"We are in the areas prepared for the children of the Eternal. All of them."

He began to walk slowly down the street so I joined him and walked in slow stride beside. I couldn't help but notice the mansions that we were passing by so casually. I recognized only some of the materials that composed their structures, but the ones I could identify were nothing less than of the utmost value. Gold, diamonds used like brick, and a silvery metal I assumed was platinum were as far as my diagnosing took me. There was no price spared on these homes, yet I never caught sight of anyone inside any of them.

"Joshua, are most of these mansions empty?"

"Yes."

"But who would be crazy enough to not dwell in such beautiful and lavish houses?"

Joshua sighed. "Many are crazy enough, or rather misled enough. It is such a waste. But not for long. Nothing I did will stay a waste. My mere *word* does not return void; surely then, my blood will not either. But just watch; it is all culminating for The Reunion." He paused, then seemed to surrender to the urge of divulging something to me rather than keeping it for another time.

"Scythe, there is still much work to be done here and in the lower lands."

I am not sure what I did with my face, but whatever it was made Joshua smile.

"You didn't think there was nothing to *do* here did you?" He said.

"Honestly, I thought that we would just adore and enjoy you."

"That is exactly what we are going to do, just not *only* in song."

"But, work? I thought that only existed as a result of The Fall. It seems *work* would have very little bearing here."

"Ah. The kind of work one does now won't be the kind that involves toiling and the sweat on your brow but the kind that when finished, one steps back to look at what they have accomplished. It is very satisfying. You will love it. And I will work with you, so you will get to do what you assumed you would do here after all."

It was a curious feeling knowing that I was going to get to work alongside Joshua doing these tasks. I had no idea what I was about to do, but the thought of doing whatever it was with Him was enough to excite me beyond rationality. Whatever we were about to do, I could do it forever, even at the threat of the possible repetition of doing it over and over for hundreds of years (I happen to thoroughly dislike most forms of repetition), yet I would be happy if I only did it with Joshua. He had the ability to transform the most mundane of situations into glorious escapades full of unexpected turns and twists. We could dig ditches together for years and I would be happy if I did it with Him. In fact, I wondered if hell would be hell if He was with me. Hell itself very well may bend in its ghastliness, possibly even break, under the influence of His Presence.

Joshua continued. "You will soon learn that this place is continually being made new. The older things are still left intact, for here the new does not replace the old but rather, compliments it. Here the preservation of the beautiful things of the past does not hinder the progression and expansion forward."

He turned in a slow circle with his arm outstretched, a finger pointing towards the horizon.

"And in these lands that happens naturally. Nobody works to make it happen, for nobody has stolen creation's ability to recreate here like they did in the lower lands. Enter The Eternal's desire. His hope is that this same process begin to take place in the lower lands. The sons of men have this task before them. They were the ones to take the earth from this inheritance, so they will be the ones to restore it."

"Are you saying that this is the work I will be doing? Restoring the earth to its former glory?" I said.

"No. I am telling you what many will do. The work you have been assigned to do is different."

"Are you going to tell me or make me guess?"

Joshua smiled. "You were always good at being frank, weren't you? I've always liked a straight forward response spoken from a transparent heart. You *are* one of my favorites, Scythe."

We both knew He had dodged the question, albeit graciously. He was very good at both parts; the dodging and the graciousness. I laughed and then said, "So no, you aren't going to tell me?"

Joshua's hands flew to the small of his back as he broke into a small fit of hysterics, his face thrown back like he was drinking from a unseen waterfall overhead, mouth wide open.

"I planned on telling you! I have a lot of ground to cover. Be patient, my friend."

I had always hated when people told me to be patient. In the world before this one people were always wanting to function at such a slow speed that when they got around me they felt I was moving too fast. I am not sure if I made them unsure of their own speed, but it seemed to threaten them, even sometimes take on a hint of jealousy. It was as though they thought that moving quickly into the things of The Eternal should be done at the slowest speed possible rather than tackled with the greatest passion and speed possible! Why delay? Being told to "be patient" became quite an irritable statement. When they would make such a statement, more than anything else it would immediately confirm my suspicion of the person's inability to just do what they should do instead of doddling around in questioning and doubt. I reasoned that if you knew something was right, do not hesitate to sprint for it. That is why Paul called it a race, not a cancer walk. I couldn't help that I worked quicker than most and usually discovered things first. It wasn't a point of pride; if anything I wished I moved at everyone else's pace so that I didn't catch flack for it; Running ahead doesn't always make you popular. But I couldn't help it. I was always running ahead of the pack, not by trying to run faster, but by running the speed that was most natural to me.

But when Joshua told me to be patient, it wasn't the same as if someone had back in the lower lands. If anyone ran faster than me into the things of the Eternal, it was Him. Thus when He said it, it was the first time I could listen. He didn't mean, "Slow down", He meant, "If you do things at my speed, you will go faster than if you tried to go faster." *That* I could listen to.

"Alright. Go ahead." I said happily, eager to oblige His request.

"The honor of being given work to do now is determined by two things, both derived from a person's life in the lower lands. First, the responsibilities that one stewarded well on that side plays a major part in what you will be doing on this side. The reason for this is because that life was simply somewhat like a brief training for this life. If someone did something well there, they will be prepared to reign in that facet of this land. For example, Agnes Bojaxhiu, or as you may know her by Teresa, has been given the joy of being mother over those that come here before the years of their life were able to be matured on earth. She is a mother to countless children here, one of the more wealthy women in our midst in fact, and all because she stewarded that gift on earth in simplicity and genuineness. Yes, her wealth is renowned here.

The second part that determines one's role in both The Abode or the lower lands is the pleasure they took in a thing. If you loved something in your life there that was worthy of affection because The Eternal's hand was in its creation, then you will have a role in its establishment and expansion here, as well as in the lower lands. For example, some gave themselves to song, not to be seen, but because they loved music itself and loved to give it away to The Eternal as a gift. That will not be disregarded or ignored, but capitalized upon. They will lead others in their love of a thing. Others had and have a deep fondness towards the Hawaiian islands, even though they are here in these uncorrupted lands; their hearts still long for the flower-laced air of that place. Thus, those that really loved the land and its culture will be trusted to enjoy it further and bring it into the newness that it is destined for. I wouldn't give the responsibility of stewardship to someone for a thing they do not have love for. Those that love what they are working at will always produce the best results. Which leads me to you, Scythe."

"Joshua, what is it that I stewarded well and enjoyed on earth?"

"Many things, which may be why you aren't sure what you will be doing. All that you enjoyed and looked after will be made use of, to your enjoyment, but for now The Eternal and I have decided upon one specific thing for you to do. Something of great importance."

"I am all ears."

"Your work will consist of doing what you did so well back on earth. Even the Seers saw this gift that you so effortlessly walked in. You were a salesman of sorts, Scythe. And I don't mean the door to door kind or the sort that one finds in used car lots. You have the ability to make someone want what they didn't think they wanted. You have the ability to accept someone where they are at and love them into a whole new place. You are like a tool for harvest. *That* is what you and I are going to do. These mansions need to be filled."

In hopes that He would explain more I stayed silent, not quite being able to connect the dots yet.

"I want my whole family to be here. I want every person that I died for to be living where I am. Do you understand what I am telling you Scythe?"

"Not in the foggiest. Who will we fill these mansions with? There is nobody left to fill them. Everyone that is supposed to be here is here now."

"Really?"

"Well I assumed so, but when you ask me questions like *that* I'm not so sure anymore." We both laughed.

I continued. "But I thought that time has been sealed up and the chasm has opened between this realm and....well, you know." I didn't want to speak its name in this holy place.

Joshua finished my incomplete sentence. "The Lands of Oblivion?"

"Is that what you call it here? Yes, I suppose that is what I am referring to."

"And are you concerned to speak of it here? No need to be apprehensive to mention it. The Eternal thinks of it often. In fact, a higher priority in His mind, even more than the sweeping and remaking of the old earth, is this issue. One *could* say that The Abode's primary objective is its opposite."

"So that place actually exists?"

"Of course. Though it isn't predominantly a place but more of a state of being. We are going to enter that state and by doing so, travel to a place far from here." As He said that He looked right at me and raised His eyebrows, smiling, the way an older brother looks at a younger brother that he is about to lead into an adventure that involves a fair amount of mischievousness.

"Are you saying that You and I are going to fill these mansions with the people that are from there?"

"That is exactly what I am saying."

I shook my head in wonder, but beaming. "Well then! Surprise, surprise. You have a lot of explaining to do. Never felt that way with You before!" I said sarcastically.

Joshua began laughing again, as did I. Usually the mental flood of unanswered questions provokes one to irritation if not anger, but the heaviest of topics couldn't diminish our capability to possess joy. Not in this place and with this Man. I had many questions but I had no doubt that Joshua would explain in the most effective way possible if given enough time. All I had to do was follow.

And again, like He read my mind, He said,

"The force that is behind the questions of 'why' and 'how' of what we are going to do is diminished if you just start with a few basic points and work from there.

I brought you to these neighborhoods so that you can understand that from the beginning of time We have been preparing a place for each and every one of Our children, not just a select few. The scriptures are very clear that I came to die *for all.* Heaven and hell are both full of forgiven sinners."

"That is an interesting doctrine." I said.

"Plain *fact* cannot be mere doctrine. To assume I died for a specific elite few is to insult my character and dishonor my sacrifice. What I did really was big enough to cover every human ever created. The secret to predestination and election is that all were predestined and elected, even before the foundations of the world were laid. All were loved. All are loved. All will be loved. Nobody can be created outside of love, for there is only One that creates. Yet, for a person to choose to *receive* the gift of my death, namely, My love, is a whole other matter altogether, and I am not delving into that right now, though we will later.

To let this wondrous land go partially uninhabited would be a waste of unprecedented proportions. This place will never be fully *itself* until that place is emptied. If one is missing, all are missing something. And this place isn't about incompletion.

But what is even more important and staggering is how The Eternal *feels* about this. Any father's heart is fragmented over a broken and scattered family until his whole family is brought back under his roof and in his care. A father, even a bad one, loves every child in his family. He even loves the rascally one, not just the few that act the way he pleases. For that reason, one can only imagine how much more *this* Father feels.

Come. It is very important that I show you not mostly what you are calling others out of, but what you are calling others into. Your ability to persuade people will come not from sowing the fear of punishment into their hearts, but by pulling out the gold in them that is already present. Then you merely point them in the direction of the land that the gold was originally mined from."

And with that, Joshua turned and began walking out of the empty neighborhood, towards the taller buildings in the distance.

Five

I followed Joshua through the streets that wove between the extravagant homes and back to The City. Upon entry, Joshua headed past the banqueting hall and towards what I assumed was more of the heart of the city, as the buildings towered even higher above us in that direction.

I began to hear the sound of water, and soon we rounded a corner and came upon a large, clear, gently moving river. It cut directly through The City, and seemed to be without any curve or variation in its direction, making its path a perfectly straight line. Straddling the water was a tree that, rather than solid matter, seemed to be made of particles of light. These bits of light were moving about and coursing through the veins of the trunk and branches like blood does in mammals. The tree glowed warmly and in a curiously independent way, as though every other light could go out because their source of energy had been cut short, but this tree would still shine forth. For a moment I thought that maybe it didn't just have its own source of power, but even that it *was* the source for everything else that gave off light. One leg of its trunk was firmly set on one side of the river and the other leg on the opposite bank. Its arms were many and extended out with its fruits available to anyone passing by, like an old man on a corner selling his farmed treasures in a crowded market. The tree was bright and happy, but had a feel of ancientness about it that caused one to take notice.

I unintentionally strayed from the direction that Joshua was leading, my attention now fixed fully on the tree. Joshua, instead of staying put where I broke off from our course and calling to me or going after me in order to drag me back on course, He just simply diverted off course as well, following behind me. It is like He knew that much like a child following their parent, it wasn't that I was not following Him when I went in the wrong direction, but had just gotten distracted by something else. He didn't interpret my change in direction as rebellious or fickle but rather as fascination. Children (and I am not referring primarily to age) are the kind that are captured by every flashing light and bright color. They are best defined by how easily they are in awe of anything that remotely resembles their Creator. This is not to be rebuked.

It seemed that Joshua didn't just tolerate this fascination, but actually liked this kind of childlikeness, for He walked up beside me under the tree and just stood there looking at it with me rather than telling me He had an agenda or a place to go and things to do. He stopped what he was doing, catering to my childlike intrigue. I think Joshua knew that there is something simple in fascination that is akin to worship, and instead of being irritated at my distraction, He bathed in my wonder like it was He that I was staring at.

"It is a fantastic tree, isn't it?" I said.

"Yes it is. We had it transplanted and brought here after Adam and Eve abandoned it for the other tree."

"Wait...This is the tree of life?"

"Yes. In fact, now that I think of it, take a few of its leaves. We may need them later."

I walked under the umbrella of branches, reached up and gently plucked a handful of leaves, then placed the leaves in a pocket of the garment that I was wearing.

"Joshua, are we able to eat the fruits?"

"Of course. Men were always invited to eat the fruit. Though you have already received Me, so the intended results of the fruits won't do anything that you don't already have.

"Which were?"

"Men were supposed to live forever in Adam's day, but they forfeited that gift for knowledge, and not the kind of knowledge that comes to a person through their heart when they talk to The Eternal in their closet. That kind of knowledge, the kind discovered in the secret place, is more about *knowing* than knowledge in the traditional use of the word. Unfortunately, the kind of knowledge that Eve and Adam forfeited abundant life for was the kind that only the brain can digest; facts and information and useless chatter. It is the type of thing men spout off to impress their friends and debate rivals in seminaries. At best it is a facade of real knowledge. True knowledge," He paused, "...is to know Someone rather than something."

"And when they ate of that facade of knowledge, what happened?"

"Well, they got something wholly different than what they thought they were getting. They received whatever remains when innocence is taken away."

"But what about what You said before...about them living forever?"

"One cannot serve two masters. They couldn't eat of both trees. It was one or the other. In their eating from the other tree, they surrendered their ability to be immortal. The fruit from this tree," He pointed up, "...enabled them to do that."

"Or they can just get to know You, right?"

"Exactly. I crafted this tree long ago. I like to work with wood. After all, I *am* a carpenter." Joshua laughed loudly at his own joke, but I had the impression He did so just because He knew it wasn't that funny. I laughed simply because He was laughing.

"So cheesy." I said while shaking my head in mock disapproval.

"Exactly. Ah! It is so good to have you here with me Scythe. How I have longed to be with you like this. I am so glad that you are here."

"Me too, Joshua."

"Well," He said while He wiped His hands together as though He had just been working in the garden and had some leftover dirt still clinging to his skin, "...shall we continue?"

"Of course."

He turned and led me back in the direction we were originally headed. It turned out we didn't have much further to go in order to reach our destination. We walked about one hundred yards from the Tree, downstream, and came upon a small dock that extended a bit into the water. Tied to the dock was a simple, but exquisite, boat. It was the type that should have oars, the way a row boat should, but had no oars and especially no sputtering outboard engine on the back; that wouldn't have suited this place at all. All it possessed were two seats on the inside, and at the tip of the bow a metal hoop through which the rope from the dock was looped. The boat was dark brown in color and seemed to be made of koa, which had been manicured so precisely that its shine made the wood like looking in a mirror. It was breathlessly perfect.

"Would you care to get in, Scythe?"

"Of course. Where are we headed?"

"We are headed to the higher regions of this land. While on the earth you had be brought low in order to be exulted, or go down to ascend up, here one must go up before they can effectively go down. You must know the joy awaiting anyone that comes here in order to effectively sell it to them and make them want it."

.

Six

I stepped into the boat, which I have to mention didn't rock from side to side like it was going to tip at all, unlike boats I had been in before that were akin to the size of this boat. Joshua got in after me, and then began to unravel the rope that was holding the boat to the dock. The moment He had the rope untied, the current of the river stole us, drifting further away from the Tree. With the Tree upstream, I wondered where we were going. I turned to see where we were headed. Glorious buildings still rose up around us with streets connecting them. The current seemed to quickly gather speed, and soon we were rushing past The City. Part of me wanted to slow down so that I could see what we were passing, as these areas of The City were all new to me, but another part of me enjoyed the speed and wanted to continue. Bridges breezed past us overhead, and Joshua leaned back on his hands, relaxing.

A very odd thing happened next. It doesn't seem odd to me now, but that is because I hadn't been here long enough to understand the lack of physical laws there are here. It started without me noticing for a few moments, because it was so natural and smooth. I was looking out at The City when I realized that the buildings didn't seem quite as tall. I looked to their tops and wondered why these towers of glory wouldn't be made quite as high as the rest of them in The City, but when I looked down in order to measure them up once again (thinking I got it wrong the first time), I realized that it wasn't that the buildings were any shorter but that I was in fact taller. I wasn't taller in the sense of bodily growth, but in the sense that the boat and the water weren't near the ground anymore. The water was no longer laying upon the crust of that heavenly land as I supposed it should be. The buildings had looked like they were lacking height because *we* had gained height. Even as I realized what was happening, our altitude continued, and we were now eye level with the tops of the highest of the buildings in the City. Let me clarify; we weren't *floating* necessarily. I reasoned that we were traveling as we had on the Day of Levitation, but the fact of the matter was that we were still in the boat, Joshua was still laying back and resting on his hands, now smiling. He seemed to be subtly enjoying my apparent incertitude about what was taking place. Since we were still in the boat, I looked to where the river was, thinking that it could explain the answers to some of my questions since it determined where we had been and were it was going. The boat still sat firmly in its current, but the river itself had no actual container around it to direct its flow, like the banks of a shore do. It was very odd to see a liquid uncontained and yet still staying together. This river seemed to go where ever it wanted, as though it was very much alive and had a will of its own. The top of the river was composed as a river normally would be in the sense that it was relatively smooth and unbroken, but its underside was much more jumbled and wild, with droplets dropping away from the main body of water and then rushing back against gravity to join the mass as it pushed us higher into the air. I had to lean over the edge of the boat to get a good look at it, and I have never been a big fan of heights, but wasn't in the least bit worried about it now. Things like falling don't occur to you here, and if they do, it is only because you know it wouldn't hurt you if you did, so you think about in the context of fun rather than fear.

The river itself was clearly headed *up*, which I had also never seen before. I had seen water start on a elevation and make its way *down*, through clouds and then mountains and to the inevitable basin of a place, but never the other way around. This water, on the other hand, was moving forward and up at a diagonal angle from the ground.

Now, that is where it seemed to be headed (up), but where we had been was just as curious. The river behind us was just as intact as it is on a normal river, and wasn't falling apart like water does when suspended in the air. I could see the steady incline we had taken, the river's point of touchdown on the ground far behind and below us, and the path we had traveled on via the river through The City.

We headed up for a short while, then started coming closer and closer to what looked to me like a ceiling of sorts. The river seemed to jet right into it but disappeared after that because the "ceiling" couldn't be seen through. It looked like the river wasn't stopped by the horizontal wall that we were heading towards, but continued to flow through it. I must admit that I wasn't fearful to what was going to happen, but also couldn't rationally conceive what exactly was going to happen when we came up against it. All I could think of when trying to recall something hitting a wall, especially at the speed we were traveling, were the old car advertisements that showed crash test dummies taking a beating in slow motion. This made Joshua giggle in the back of the boat, as He was undoubtedly aware of my thought.

"Here we go!" He said, as He firmly grabbed the sides of the boat with His hands, like He was anticipating some kind of extreme situation to unfold momentarily. I followed suite and grabbed the sides of the boat.

We hit that ceiling with such speed that I barely recognized the moment before from the moment after. There was no crash, not even a jostle. I looked back at Joshua and gave Him the most patronizing look I could muster up, but couldn't help but break into laughter as well. I had been had. And Joshua 's laughter wasn't just aimed at the fact that He had grabbed the sides of the boat to dupe me into thinking we were about to crash, but He was actually laughing *at me*. His laughing at me may sound odd, as though it is unkind to laugh at someone in *any* situation, but I felt thoroughly enjoyed by Him when He did it. In fact, "any situation" doesn't really apply to Him. He is in a category of His own. The essence behind what He does isn't determined by what we think we know of that action from when another did it. Rather, what He does is always determined by who He is. And it is always loving and kind and gracious and thoughtful and understanding and so on. He does not know how to mock or be cruel, but He does know how to have fun.

"That was crazy!" I blurted out. "Thanks for the warning!" I said sarcastically.

"You were brilliant. The Abode is a wild place, but in no way at all bad. Much like this place; welcome to The Refulgence."

Seven

I hadn't noticed, probably because of the distraction that came from our entry, but the light was recognizably brighter now. It wasn't that The Abode wasn't completely bright, because it was. In fact, I would say that it is a *far* brighter place than any light ever created for the world the earth consisted in. It was just that this place had even more light, somehow.

In fact, this light made all light I had seen before look dim, though only when the two were side by side and being compared, otherwise one would never know there could be anything more radiant that what they were beholding.

Now though, I was beholding something very different. Joshua seemed quite fine but I couldn't help but feel something of a squirming inside of me. It wasn't that what I was feeling wasn't *good* in every possible way, but that I wasn't particularly accustomed to this higher level and the brightness it possessed. It became quickly clear to me that while I had become relatively comfortable with the light in The Abode, I wasn't yet totally ready to inhabit this place like I could there. I had a great sense that there were places in me, though I had been made perfect (and not just when I entered The Abode, but thousands of years before due to Joshua and

The Great Sacrifice), that still had much need of maturing, and as that work took place I would feel just as comfortable here as I do in The Abode.

The only way I can put it into perspective is how one feels when they go from living in a colder climate to one that is located in the tropics. It isn't that they don't have light in the colder climate, but that the new climate has even more of it. Their skin takes time to adjust to the new measure of ultraviolet rays of heat, and at first it may result in an uncomfortable burn if they don't inch into it slowly and allow their skin to mature and get used to the new atmosphere and light. In this place though, one's body isn't harmed in any way (for that is impossible), but one's spirit does feel the increase of sheer *goodness* in this place. When a person's spirit has been accustomed for so long to places of mixture, where there is good along with bad, the intensity of this newfound purity strikes one's spirit suddenly, making it gasp in wonder and shock.

It isn't that The Abode has any mixture in it, but that the essence of goodness was even more unveiled here than it is there. This place made my inner man lurch with joy, tremble over the unavoidable beams of goodness that pierced through it, and burn with the fire that comes from the flame of love. It was fantastic, but the kind that also causes one to lose consciousness or faint if they don't monitor themselves carefully.

The river had leveled out once more, again grounded against the terrain. We were quickly coming up on a dock to our right, and Joshua extended His right arm like a hook to snag it. He easily took hold of the dock as it went rushing past, and the boat quickly became motionless on the water, like the current suddenly decided to ignore the vessel completely. Joshua stepped out of the boat and onto the dock, turned, and extended out His hand to help me out of the skiff.

It was when Joshua helped me out of the boat that I noticed that the light was mostly emanating from a certain direction quite a distance away. This became clear to me not just because you could look out at the horizon and discern a distinct rush of light coming from a specific bearing, but because when Joshua stood between myself and the centrality of the light I felt as one does when they slip on sunglasses in the sunshine after the glare of the light has momentarily blinded you while driving on the freeway. I would ease up a bit when He was standing in just the right spot, and when He would shift out of that place I would cover my face and eyes with my hands like one does when someone flips on a light after their eyes have adjusted to the darkness of a room. Joshua didn't cast any shadow, like you would suppose, so it wasn't that He was shielding me from the source of light in the distance; He had no need to protect me from anything because there wasn't anything hurting me. Instead of me hiding in His shadow, it was that when I looked at the light *through* Him it was comprehendible to me. It was then that my being was more able to apprehend it and embrace it. Otherwise it was too foreign for me to digest it in spirit, mind, or body. It wasn't that I didn't like it, but that it was of an essence thoroughly unalike anything I had beheld before, distinctly set apart.

There were many people in that place, and they didn't come across any more spiritual than people were in The Abode, but just simply seemed to like it here more. I didn't pick up on there being a theme of this level being more of a spiritually elite than those in the place we had just come from. Rather it seemed that each had a personal preference and some chose to live below, and some even higher above, as I would soon discover. The difference between the levels was the variance of light and the overall setting. This place looked very different in comparison to The Abode. While The Abode had a feel of ancientness and royalty, The Refulgence felt very tidy and succinct, with a feel of advancement somehow, like it was familiar with the future rather than the past. There were still growing things of nature, but they looked less wild and more cultivated, and I wondered as I walked by them if they were even possibly engineered. All surfaces were smooth and polished, and you had the distinct feeling of symmetry and intentionality as you walked about the place. Just as The Abode had been wild but not bad or dangerous, this place was orderly but in no way controlled. It was not without the liberty to be disorderly or undignified if one so desired to be. I didn't feel as though I needed to *behave*, as one does when they walk into a place that is uncluttered, and I knew that if I wanted to, I could roll around in the grass as a horse does when it is enjoying itself, or make a mess and nobody would mind in the slightest.

Joshua took me towards the light, and we walked for no short time. It felt like we were walking into the sun itself from the start, and that feeling only multiplied in intensity every step closer we got. Soon we were close enough to see (not because of distance but because of the light) that we were on the outskirts of another city. Joshua lead me to the center of it, to a structure that shined brighter than all the others, and walked inside.

There was no doubt that the building was enormous when looked at from the outside, but the odd thing is that when you got inside, it was obviously much bigger than you first thought. The room we stood in was about 200 yards wide, completely empty, and so long that I couldn't see the back wall. I concluded that I must have gotten the proportions on the outside wrong on my first take, but later learned in these lands, the size of a structure on the outside didn't necessarily determine the size on its inside. Things are like that here; they don't make sense to the natural mind. We all grew up with a certain way of thinking, then were fed with books that reinforced all of those facts and laws even further; facts and laws we assumed would always be concrete and staying rather than shifting, bending, and sometimes even breaking. Then you get here and realize that earth was just one way of doing things, and that The Designer has many ways to of doing things. To a learned mind like mine, which immediately qualified me to be placed in the category of unlearned, this place was wonderfully confounding.

On one end of the room there were three thrones, and in the largest throne sat a man that I hadn't seen before, wherefrom the light that was so blindingly magnificent obviously radiated from. My first thought upon seeing him was more of a question, wondering how the throne that he sat in and the two on either side of him didn't just melt away into nothingness because of the power of the light that came from him. He was beautiful.

"Is that, you know, one of the ministering spirits that serve You?"

"No. This is who I serve."

"This is....?" My voice trailed off involuntarily.

"Yes."

I was surprised at Joshua's lack of preparation for this moment. Maybe it was because He knew that I could now be around The Eternal anytime I desired, but still; this was the One that I had desired to behold for as long as I could remember, even before I knew Him by name. This was possibly the greatest moment of my existence, and suddenly it was upon me with a suddenness like a lion on prey. Maybe Joshua didn't prepare me ahead of time because I would have shied away from it or prepared some kind of speech rather than just be myself. It didn't matter now, because Joshua had taken my hand and led me before Him before I could think of what to say or how to communicate the years of love that I had stored up in my heart to give to Him.

He was sitting on His throne, and I was about to open my mouth to start fumbling around, no doubt in hopes of trying to win His approval (though it was already mine), or to try to make a good first impression. But before I could try to be slick or impressionable, He was up and out of His seat and wrapped around me, lifting me into the air, laughing like I had never heard someone laugh. He was in front of me, around me, inside me, below me, and above me all at once. He was everything.

I became completely undone. I already had no pain in my heart to surrender through tears, but they flowed like I did nonetheless. There is a certain ache that one carries, an ache deeper than pain, one of desire, that is only quenched when the focus of your heart is finally and fully yours.

He didn't say much. He didn't need to. His laughter over me told me everything I needed to know: He was proud of me, He knew everything about me, He understood me, He loved me more than I would ever discover, and most of all, He really liked me.

What surprised me was that He made me feel the exact way that Joshua did. His presence was so akin to Joshua's, His smell and embrace so precisely Joshua's, that it became clear to me that I would have a difficult time distinguishing between their hearts and personality. They looked different physically, obviously, but they felt alike and had the same *nature* about them. Actually, they weren't just similar, they were exactly the same. They may even be the same Person while somehow being two separate Beings.

While in His embrace it occurred to me almost instantly that He would never do something that Joshua wouldn't do, and Joshua I knew would never harm me in any form or manner. I reckoned that Joshua would rather die than hurt me in the slightest. And since Joshua was serving The Eternal rather than primarily the other way around, Joshua must be the way He was because of the heart of The One holding me. I thought Joshua reflected The Eternal, and He does, but I realized that equally, if not more, Joshua is the way He is because The Eternal is that way. If this was true, and I sensed it was, how I had misunderstood The Eternal all of my life and up until this moment!

I felt Him unwrap Himself from me and step back as He pointed to the throne that was to the right of the center throne.

"Would you honor us with your presence?"

"Of course, my king." I was at ease, but spoke with the utmost reverence towards this Being of Light. He was so worthy of everything I could give, and everything I couldn't.

I sat on the plush throne, wondering whose place of authority I was usurping, as though they may walk into the room and demand for me to take my rightful place, which was not there on *that* throne. I knew that there were three of Them, and wondered if the Spirit would become visible and quietly and gently correct me.

Joshua took His seat on the throne on the other side of the center seat, but the Father did not sit. Instead He disappeared into a door behind us, and reappeared a moments later with grapes in one hand, and a fan in the other. I stood and outstretched my hands to take the grapes and fan, but the Father motioned me to sit again.

Then, to my wonder, the Eternal kneeled next to the throne I sat upon and began lightly fanning me and slowly feeding me grapes. I must admit this made me extremely uncomfortable. Wasn't I supposed to serve Him rather than Him serve me? This could not be. Was it a test? I reached out for the clump of grapes and the fan, but the Eternal actually dodged my grabby movement, smiling.

"Scythe, just receive. I know you want to serve Me, but a father's job is to lead his family. To Me, leading looks more like serving than it does giving out commands or lording power over everyone else. Let me lead you."

When He tells you to do something, everything in you wants to obey Him, not because if you don't you are rebellious or loveless, but because you know you can trust that what He says He only says because He has your best intentions in mind. I relaxed and literally had to tell myself to just *let go;* It was fully a conscious decision I had to make and continue to make every time He fanned me or fed me a grape. It was so hard not to *do* anything.

"Everything good always started with Me doing it first. You are able to love because I first loved you. You can only give away what you have first received."

I thought for a moment. "But surely You have already served me."

"True. But I love to keep doing it. I don't do this because this is the noble thing to do, but because I can't help but do it. This is who I am."

"I am very sorry but this isn't what I expected at all!" I said, bewildered.

"I am sure. And I understand. Humans seem to think they possess the ability to give without first being given to, but they don't. They are more dependent upon Me than that."

It felt like His spoiling me went on forever, though it probably wasn't very long at all. He only stopped after I finally felt the last hesitation leave that kept me from fully delving into thinking about what was actually happening. When I let it pierce me, it went deep, irrevocably deep. I felt my capacity to love extend and grow, not only for Him, but for everyone.

The Eternal finally sat down on the throne next to me, all the grapes eaten, and folded up the fan. With His left hand He took my right hand gently and held it. I sat there just staring in awe at our two hands that overlapped one another. This was all too much to compute, maybe because I expected this place, especially my interactions with Him, to be all about me giving to Him, not Him giving to me, and definitely in a corporate setting. To have Him alone was enough to completely ruin me, and to have Him *serve* me was inexplicable, but to touch Him like this (with such casual lingering) caused me to become rapturous. Like a broken record or a man that has lost his mind, I kept saying over and over in my head and possibly out loud as well, "I am touching the Eternal. I am touching the Eternal. I am touching the Eternal." Maybe I felt the need to repeat it over and over because it was so hard to believe that it was actually happening.

The Eternal was entertained by my reaction to His actions. He would see my surprise or elation and roar with laugher. I had never felt so enjoyed, and I wasn't doing a thing.

Joshua stood, vanished through the door behind us, and returned with a golden basin full of water. He stopped in front of me, stooped down, and set the bowl on the ground next to where I sat. He then preceded to wash my feet and dry them with His clothes.

I had heard of a story much like what Joshua was doing now, one from the holy writs that took place years long past, but experiencing it first-hand caused me to realize how little I believed, or rather understood, exactly what took place in that passage. Maybe it was the fact that we were in The Refulgence rather than a dingy, dirt encrusted house, thus all the more annunciating the stark reality that He is divine and I am not but *He* is the one down on His knees doing something that is only fitting for a slave to do to a master. Yet, there we were.

One becomes quite humble upon entry of these countries; It is natural when one sees how little they are and nevertheless how largely they are loved. But this was a whole new ambuscading of humility upon my heart. It stormed into me like the advancing front lines of some great battle and took up residence within my boarders. Humility is knowing exactly who you are in light of who He is, and I felt it. I saw myself as I really was. I was minuscule and enormous at the same time, in all beautiful ways. My smallness was such a relief, and my greatness was only because of Him, which also resulted in relief.

Joshua kneeled at my feet for quite some time, then rose, took the bowl away, and returned and sat upon His throne, at The Eternal's right side.

Thoughts like, "Why am I sitting with them? Why am I also on a throne?" kept rushing through my head.

And though they both assuredly heard my questions, they did not respond to them but rather The Eternal said, "They cannot help but come. Desire has become too great."

And with those words, what I would estimate as millions of people, ages and ages of them, instantly appeared in front of us in the empty room.

Eight

They did not hesitate. Immediately, such chorus of adoration and affection rose up from their midst that it shook the building. They may have each been singing their own song, or maybe it was the same song, I couldn't tell. It was possible that it was both, where individual songs weave together to make a greater song, like how song leaders sometimes break a group into parts to sing rounds, each part harmonizing with the others, only if that was what was happening here, it was millions of rounds weaving with one another at the same time. Regardless, the sound was like verbal silk; smooth, comforting, and beautiful. Notes that I had never heard before came to life, like they had found notes between the notes I was accustomed to. The bare walls of the room were now acting like soil, though they were strictly composed of wood and stone; the song caused vines and flowers to sprout from their hard surface and crawl down the walls, as though the plants couldn't help but come to life once the music collided with the air. The ceiling was alive with creatures of beauty and wonder that I had never seen before, some stuck to the ceiling and walking about upside down like gravity had been reversed, others flying. The entire room had become incredibly full and alive in a matter of seconds.

And while I could have looked about forever, studying and gaping at the sights in front of me and around me, I looked to my right at The Eternal to see how He was responding to this reverence. The light coming from The Eternal was deafeningly bright when I had first come into the room, but now it seemed even more invasive and strong, as though the song accentuated it further moment by moment. It was building. I wasn't scared by this, but wondered what would happen to everything around Him, including myself, if this continued. The Eternal was so gentle and gracious and thoughtful in everything I had seen Him do so far, but I couldn't help but think that if He wanted to, all of this light could engulf not just His throne and the people and the room, but *everything*. And I don't just mean it could swallow up this world, but every world. If He weren't good, and only motivated by love, surely this power that came from Him would have already vaporized every material and spiritual thing that exists. All that would be left standing would be *Him*, surrounded by nothingness. He is like standing in the middle of a nuclear bomb being detonated, but coming out unharmed. He is sheer power that is completely safe.

And yet while I was thinking this through, I began to notice that the light was starting to take a toll on The Eternal's throne, specifically the area of the throne His back was up against and the portion of the armrest that His limbs where stretched over. The throne was emanating what I believed to be smoke, for I smelled it before I really saw it. It smelled like lavender, but more milky and sweet, and not at all like what you would call normal smoke. Within three or four seconds the throne was visibly smoking. It wasn't on fire, and I couldn't feel heat, but it was obviously under some kind of influence due to the light. After another short span of time, I could see the same effect on my own arm, then on those singing out in front of us, and soon everything was giving forth this fragranced smoke. The smoke was slowly filling this temple of sorts that we were within.

Joshua must have gotten up from His seat because He was suddenly standing in front of me, the stuff now thick all around us, and He said, "Inhale."

I took a deep breath and watched the smoke move into my mouth from all around me like it was being both chased and lured into my lungs by some unseen force. Here one doesn't need air like we did before so breathing isn't so much an involuntary action as much as a voluntary one, but when I did exhale so that I could take another breath, a feeling of peace erupted throughout me, starting in my head and lungs and rippling through my body like liquid waves. It was so recognizable and unmistakable that it felt like I may simply disappear, ceasing to be present and instead appear some other place that was even more quintessentially tranquil than the room I was standing in, if such a place exists. This apprehending placidity immediately caused my eyelids to wrap themselves over my eyes in order to insure the maximum amount of pleasure to come out of that moment.

To my surprise, when I opened my eyes the room was gone. The Eternal was no longer to my right, but Joshua still stood in front of me. We were somewhere else altogether.

I was a bit shocked and displaced. "Where are we? Where did the Eternal go?"

"He is always near. We are in the country above The Refulgence. It is called The Spectrum."

"How did we get here? Did the smoke take us here?"

"Yes. Smoke has always been able to take people into other dimensions, though men used it in its counterfeit version on earth rather than the way it was intended here. There are many ways to every country."

My mind was still reeling from the distinct shift from being so inebriated by peace, then coming into a different place altogether. "Speaking of that..." I said dazedly, "...how many countries are there?"

"The Countries of Matrimony go as far up as one desires to go."

"Is that what this world is called? The Countries of Matrimony?

Joshua looked pleased. "There is no name that is more fitting for the purpose and fulfillment of this world. Yes."

I spoke slowly, still trying to understand. "But The Eternal's throne is on the second, uh, level, or I mean, country? If so, that is where I will settle down."

"Ah, that old, linear thinking again." Joshua said gently as He smiled. "No, The Eternal's throne is not in one country, but all. It is the same throne, but in each separate country at the same time. He can be anywhere and everywhere at once, which is why you were able to establish His throne even on earth when you manifested the fruits of this kingdom. One can find Him on His throne in The Abode just as they can in The Spectrum. Different countries, same throne."

My mind was trying to catch up, questions still raining down on me. "And what happened back there? Did He destroy all of it? Everything was smoking like it was about to implode!"

"No. He merely allowed Himself to be seen for a moment, and only a fraction of Himself at that. He *is* light. Nothing was destroyed for He cannot destroy. That role has already been filled. We could go back there now and see the room and people and thrones and they wouldn't be mangled and distraught but better than before. That is all He is capable of doing: He only makes things better. Everything smoked because it merely witnessed His being and became more like Him. The people and the items present weren't *refined* like metal was on earth with heat, for there are no impurities to be swept away now, but they *were* recreated altogether in that moment. They were going from glory to glory, whether it was a person, or a creature, or a throne. All is made new each moment they are in His presence. This is how we become more like Him; we behold Him."

We were standing in unapproachable light. All colors vividly melded together, making everything white but also visibly containing every shade possible. It occurred to me that this may be why Joshua had referred to it as The Spectrum.

In my mind, nothing could have topped the brightness of The Refulgence, but this place did with ease. The light here was the way someone feels when they have just come inside from a cold day and run a bath a bit too warm for the skin. One gets in and it feels wonderful, but they also can't help but sink in ever so slowly with wide-eyes and pressed lips. As they stay in the water they get used to it until they eventually melt into it. In similar fashion, every moment longer I was in The Spectrum I got used to the radiance. Its influence was growing and rooting into me moment by moment, changing me. As I had realized before, it didn't hurt but caused me discomfort like one experiences when they workout; It feels good and strenuous at the same time. I knew this was good, but that doesn't mean it was particularly easy.

Again, there was a direction from which the light was brightest, which I now knew was most likely the direction to the location of the throne in this country. I immediately lined myself up behind Joshua, as it was too much for me if I stepped out from behind Him. I was using Him like one uses an umbrella in a rainstorm that is combined with wind, when drops of water are flying at you horizontally. I kept Him out in front of me and paid attention that I stayed positioned behind Him. The light was so arresting that I would have thought it could have hurt or killed me if I didn't regard it through Joshua, even though I was sure that The Eternal would not just never do such a thing or allow such a thing to happen, but couldn't.

And that is the curious thing.

In that moment it became clear that Joshua is the lens we have to behold the glory of The Eternal through or we forget who The Eternal is. Even if we just experienced His heart and love for us and we know He would never harm us, it is as though we, being human, even perfected human, are still so dissimilar to Him that we need a constant reminder who He is so that we don't relapse back to thinking He is who *we* think He is. It seemed that one could fail to recall who the Eternal is unless they view Him through Joshua because of the unexplainable glory that rushes out from Him. It is so *otherworldly* to behold Him that we can easily interpret Him through our understanding rather than letting Him define Himself. I had just been with Him and witnessed His gentle goodness, but this light was so strong that it could be very easy to assume something of Him that was not true, even in this place. Thus I had to look to Joshua for clarity; The Divine made human. The Clarification.

Maybe it is shortsighted of us, but we can only have things put into context by that which we can relate to. An ant can understand another ant but cannot understand the concept of a human. The ant has no paradigm for say, getting in the car to shop for groceries or rocking an infant to sleep as one sings a lullaby over them. These things are sheer foreignness to an ant; Ants can only understand ant-like things, just as a human can really only understand human-like things. As it turns out, the ant trying to grasp who a human is happens to be not unlike men trying to understand the essence of a Being that is *composed* of light; physical and natural and spiritual all wrapped up into one matter. By no means am I inferring that we don't come to know Him fully, but that it is a journey we take over the span of forever. This is why we must look to Joshua for the exact representation of who The Eternal is, for Joshua is the Divine Human. Otherwise, we come to conclusions about The Eternal that are incorrect, and as history proves itself, that can be disastrous.

There is another reality at play as well. Everything we know and know of is simply an imitation of something that is in Him, whether an accurate imitation or one that is a counterfeit and far from the nature of the original. Many of the things that we have come to know as fearful or harmful or evil, we view in that way because of our experience of them on earth. But before they became distorted they existed within Him and were always and only good, and always and only used for good. The tricky part about that is that He goes on being Himself with no concern of changing for anyone, and you may walk up when He is doing something good and yet interpret it as fearful, or even evil, because your understanding of the thing He is doing is so rooted in what used to be rather than what is, and always was.

For example, a lion's roar is generally understood to be a warning that a maiming may take place if one doesn't back off. At worst, a gruesome death. But when He roared, it was laughter. When He laughed, it was a roar. It didn't just make your hair stand on end but also placed peace inside you. And one's hair didn't stand on end because you thought He may devour you, but because the roar still possessed every ounce of power in it that it does when a lion releases it. For hair can stand on end from awe, altogether devoid of fear.

Thus, I assume that if one didn't know Him and walked up as He laughed they could think He was communicating a warming of a maiming if one's actions didn't change, or even a gruesome death, *rather than* the actual truth; loving delight. His roar was joy; I knew because He laughed over me when I saw Him and it was nothing short of a vibrating, earth-shaking roar. It demonstrated the strength and raw power resolute within joy; a joy that caused both His enemies to flee from Him and His children to run to Him.

This explains how some of His qualities have been misperceived by men through the centuries. Priests of old used to think they needed to tie a rope to their leg when they were going to go meet with Him so that if they were struck dead they could be pulled out like a fish hooked on the end of a fishing line. I now understood that this is why. His glory is incomprehensible and misunderstood if it is not approached and sized up in the context of His nature; love. Men have seen Him as He is and turned around to proclaim that He is very thing that He is not. And this is understandable, for an ant cannot do much to correctly describe something so superior.

As we stood in this new country, out of the cloud which was not a cloud at all but material light, came a figure. Visibility was limited, like one experiences when diving in the ocean, as liquid is harder to see through than air, and I only started to make out who it was once they were a mere twenty feet away.

It was Echelon.

I turned to Joshua in wonder. He was beaming.

"Echelon!" I squealed, and ran to him. He caught me in my sprint, both of us wrapping our arms around each other in a large embrace.

"Scythe. Hello!" He burst out. He was practically bouncing with excitement, as was I.

Right off I realized that Echelon looked very different than he had when we had been on the earth. He was youthful, energetic, and just plain sensationally beauteous.

I took a step back and surveyed him, my eyes starting at his feet and making their way to his head. "Echelon, you look very different."

His eyebrows raised and he made a face of mimic surprise. "Really? Have I lost weight?"

We laughed at his joke, then I said seriously, "But really. Joshua, why does he look so unlike what he did before?"

You would think there were other things to talk about, but I was oddly stuck on Echelon's physical appearance. In reality what I was really wondering was if I looked as different and as good as he did.

"People become themselves here; who they were initially created to be. In fact, The Eternal doesn't limit how much beauty and power and glory that they can possess. Some creatures and humans are so glorious here that they can choose to believe they are more glorious than The Eternal Himself. It has happened before."

"Yes it has." Echelon interjected.

"More glorious than The Eternal?" I said in disbelief.

"Well, It isn't true of course, but it is understandable how they came to that conclusion when you see them. The Eternal doesn't control, in the least bit, how much one can have. He isn't threatened by other's splendor and magnificence. In fact, He freely hands it out. He loves to limitlessly give."

Echelon talked for a bit about how Joshua had led him to The Spectrum and about those that he had met so far in his time there. He spent most of that time talking about being reunited with his family, who had been brutally murdered before his own eyes when he was young in the lower lands. He was overjoyed at getting to know his own father and mother, two sisters, and brother. He said that he discovered more who he was by being with them, and that his father still had things to teach him. He said that though many years had been lost to death, it was all made up for in this place, plus much more.

Echelon also mentioned what he would be doing here. Not surprisingly, The Eternal, Joshua, and the Matchmaker had decided to nominate Echelon to lead groups down to the remaking of the earth. He was a very good leader and it suited him. I had the inclination to invite him along with Joshua and I, for whatever we were going to do (which I was still unclear on pertaining to specifics), but realized that if Joshua wanted him to come, He would ask Echelon Himself, so I refrained.

As Joshua and Echelon talked about some details relating to his trip to the new earth, I looked about, now able to see a bit further into the light and through its near liquid-like state. I could see people walking around, and not just people, but some that looked like giants. Others weren't large, but small and unhuman. I couldn't see all the details of their physical makeup, but from the distance I stood and with what I could gather from there, it seemed that each and every one of them looked rather perfect. Most looked as though they had rippling muscles, glossy hair that bounced or waved in the air as they walked, and some sort of attire that was monarchical in some way. They too caused me to wonder how I looked, and if I compared to their flawlessness in the slightest.

After Joshua and Echelon finished their conversation Joshua told me it was time for us to go, so I hugged Echelon goodbye and he strode off into the thickness, disappearing from view after a short while.

"Where are we going now?" I asked inquisitively.

"The Lands of Ecstasy. I will take you as high as you wish." And as soon as He had finished His sentence, we were there. We traveled as easy as how one recalls a pleasant memory; once we thought of a place, we appeared there. I had no idea where we were going therefore could not recall it or steer my way there, but Joshua had a way of gathering me with Him, and I found myself standing in this next country beside Him.

There isn't much to describe about this place, not because it isn't, I'm sure, in every way shatteringly fantastic, but because upon the very moment of our arrival we turned around and came back immediately, per my request. Even with Joshua in front of me, the light was too bright for me. Not only was the light strong, but the surroundings seemed to reflect the light, causing it to come from every direction *and* accentuate its force. For the brief moment I was there, I thought that I saw everything covered in a white substance, which would explain the aspect of reflection. If I am honest it looked like snow, draped over everything like a blanket, but the air was not cold enough to accommodate snow, at least not the kind of snow I had known. I would make a guess to say that it was in fact snow, just snow that was as it was firstly intended.

The thought went through my mind that even if the places of darkness below possessed tormenting fire as I had heard, it would never compare to the power of the wondrous light and burning of that place. Whatever burning the places of darkness had, they were merely a type and shadow of the real thing found in the more elevated levels here, above. A twisted, distorted shadow, but a shadow nonetheless. It was odd to me that even the fire of the places of darkness are a counterfeit of the real; that fire was once a very pure and harmless thing. The burning below was intended for pain, but I fled from the burning of the light in the upper regions of the Countries of Matrimony not because of pain, but because the *goodness* of it was too much to assimilate. This is the reality of love; it comes to a point where it causes one to shy away, even take to one's heels, because it is too wonderful, too apprehending, too inclusive. One begs for it to stop, for it feels that if it continued they may never come back from whatever place it is taking them. Wave after wave bears down on one's soul, and soon it feels like they will drown in pleasure if the tide doesn't change direction. But He is not one to cease. This, as Joshua later explained, was exactly the same strategy They used for the world below the world.

Nine

"What do you mean we are going there?" I blurted out. "I just got used to going up! Now I have to adjust to going down?"

"It will be an adventure!" Joshua declared, with one hand raised in a fist, pumping it back and forth in the air both victoriously and satirically, while laughing.

Joshua had just alluded to more of what He and I were going to do, but didn't give any real specifics or details. As I had learned from previous experiences, Joshua wasn't the type to only set out after everyone's questions were answered. He seemed to *prefer* to set out amidst looming questions, as though they didn't disqualify the challenge and adventure in the least (like they do for many) but instead amplified the awaiting challenge and adventure further, giving even more reason to go. He knew that unanswered questions would be clarified with time if He was alongside me.

I couldn't fathom what we were about to do, at least what I had surmised what we were about to do, for it still wasn't completely spelled out in my mind. In fact, it didn't make *any* sense to me. Leave this place to go to the place I had been counseled all of my life to steer away from? It was ludicrous to me, but I reasoned that Joshua must have some sort of logic up His sleeve that I was unaware of.

We were back in the Abode, and making our way out of The City, down the same streets we had walked when we first arrived. Assuming we would make our way all the way out of The City, I was slightly taken back when Joshua curtly stopped and pivoted on one foot as He swung open a nearby door that we were about to pass. The door was on the side of one of the towering, ancient buildings that we had been striding past, and Joshua nobly motioned me inside with one hand.

"You need a sword, Scythe." He said as I walked past him and through the door. I frowned in incertitude, not understanding why this would be true and wondering if Joshua was just pulling my leg.

The room was slightly darker than outside, lit with burning torches on the wall that burned bright blue. All along the walls hung bright and shining swords, beaming with radiance. The reflection of the torches on the blades caused blue specks of light to dance around on the walls of the room, producing a fantastic light show that didn't seem to have an end in sight. There was a man seated behind a glass counter that was stock full of small and long blades, each unique and differently styled. The man looked weathered yet joyful, as though he had seen storms but sailed through them intact. He had long, white hair and a fatherly glow in his light blue eyes. The creases in his skin around his mouth and upon his forehead caused me to feel an odd sense of affection towards him, a feeling not unlike what I had felt towards my own father in my past life.

"Hello my friend. How are you?" asked Joshua.

"I am well, my Lord. It is very good to see you. I am so glad you came by. Are you needing a blade for Scythe?" said the man.

"Yes, we are. Any recommendations?" said Joshua.

"Ah, yes." said the man, as he reached under the glass of the counter, grabbed a sword, and placed it on top of the counter for us to see.

"How do you know my name?" I asked abruptly and off topic, for I had never met this man before.

"Everyone here knows of those that have recently entered this land, as well as those yet to enter. We heartily celebrate each one that comes in, taking..." he trailed off, thinking hard, then seemed to regain himself, "...I suppose you would say "weeks" in time language, to revere what Joshua has done and the addition of the one entering. How do you like the blade?"

I had been watching this man's face closely as he spoke, somewhat mesmerized by his strangely familiar features, as though I knew him but had never met him face to face. I looked down and saw the sword in detail for the first time. It had a handle that was jet black, as though sculptured from a solid piece of ebony. The blade was silver like steel, but I thought I saw it *move* for a moment, and my eyebrows raised, wondering first why it moved and second, questioning the integrity of the metal.

"Ah! You saw that, eh?" the man said excitedly as he chuckled. "This is one of my favorites. Don't think that this is anything like what they had in your world. The blade is made from a substance that *looks* like metal, but much stronger and wiser than metal. It is part liquid."

"Granted, I don't know why Joshua is wanting me to get a blade," I said as I looked at Joshua questioningly, "but how on earth will a part liquid blade do me any good?"

The fatherly man smiled. "On *earth* it wouldn't do you any good, you are correct, at least if it was used in the barbaric way men did with swords there. But you aren't on earth, are you?"

I picked up the sword and was surprised how lightweight it was. I had my hand grasped around the hilt and if it wasn't for the pressure I was applying with my grip and my eyes fixed on it, I would have been completely unaware that I was holding a sword at all. It had the weight of air, which made my whipping it dangerously around the room very easy to do, which I immediately did by accident. To my horror, as I turned to show the blade to Joshua, I swished the sword directly towards the man behind the counter, and before I could change the direction of my movement, the sword had plunged into the neck of the man. As though the sword had shocked me or carried a contagious disease upon it, I dropped it in utter panic and disbelief as to what I had just done, closing my eyes to shield my vision from seeing the atrocity I had just effected, assuming I had just committed the first murder in The Abode.

Loud laughter from Joshua and the man caused me to open my eyes again almost immediately. The man was still seated behind the counter, appearing to be completely unharmed.

"The weight comes as a surprise to most the first time they hold it." the man explained. "This is one reason why it is part liquid. It acts as a splash of water to things it isn't meant to cut. To everything else, it cuts like tungsten. It never needs sharpening, as it immediately shapes itself after a swipe to the sharpest edge possible. Deadly, but completely safe. It is wisely dangerous." he said proudly.

"Excellent design, my friend!" Joshua said, as he reached across the counter and patted the man on the back. The man beamed as Joshua did so, as though Joshua's congratulations meant more to him than any compliment ever paid him.

I still wasn't sure why I needed a sword to begin with. It seemed to me that Joshua was readying me for some kind of battle, which didn't seem fitting to Him, nor fitting to The Abode.

"Why do I need this weapon?" I asked. "Who am I going to need to fight with this, or defend myself from?" I was already uncertain about the details that were entailed within the "adventure" we were about to take, and the addition of a sword that was "deadly" didn't calm my hesitations in the least bit.

Joshua and the man looked at one another and smiled, as though they knew something that I didn't.

Joshua said jovially to the man, "At least he asked and didn't go cutting the first ear off that he came across!"

In return the man howled in laughter, saying "Well, he almost took my head off! Give him a chance and he may take more than an ear!" Joshua followed suit in hysterics and the two of them were soon falling over each other holding their sides. I watched them unhumorously at first, then because I had been slowly infected by their joy, began to quietly giggle to myself at their silliness. After a few minutes they both righted themselves, standing up straight and wiping away the tears in their eyes.

Joshua hugged the man and then walked to the door, opened it, and like a gentleman on a first date, waved me towards the door. As I walked by Him He whisked a baldric over my head and slipped the sword into it, girding it upon my side, then reached up and grabbed a blade that was hanging on the wall closest to the door and secured it on his side as well.

Before the door to the shop closed, Joshua called back, "My friend, thank you for loving me and for feeding my sheep so fantastically well."

The man smiled contentedly in return.

Ten

Joshua wasn't walking fast, but He wasn't dawdling about either. He seemed to know exactly where we needed to go and was set on getting there sooner than later. I kept in step beside him as we past the last of the shining buildings and out into the wildness of grass, and past the long lined scar in the ground from the walls and gates that were removed. I wasn't totally sure where we had first entered, but was remotely confident that we were much further into the wildness than our entry point, moving further and further away from The City in a direction that comprised a landscape I was totally unfamiliar with.

With our back to The City we came upon a tangled mass, of vines, shrubs, trees, and branches, almost thick enough to be considered a wall. Nowhere else around us did the foliage seem so clustered except in this particular spot, and it was so unusual that it was as though it was somehow intentional. I reasoned that possibly instead, maybe there was an exceptional source of water below the ground that was feeding the plants and trees and caused them to grow in this spot more furiously than anywhere else.

"Ah, here we are. This is the entrance." Joshua said.

"Entrance to what?" I asked, not seeing any entrance at all.

"The Lands of Oblivion." Joshua said calmly.

Then without warning, Joshua took out His sword and began violently whipping it back and forth, hacking away at the heavy growth in front of us. After a few moments He stopped to catch His breath, looked back and me and said, "Come and help me?"

I must admit I was keen to try out my new sword. I was surprised how effortless it was to take down anything in its path, whether tree trunk or vine. I couldn't feel the swords weight, but also couldn't feel the resistance one feels when cutting through something, the lack thereof probably due to the blade's perfect edge. It cut material as simply as a hand cuts through the air. Within a short time we had the mass of vegetation leveled and beat back, though I couldn't help but want to go on cutting down everything in sight because of how much fun it was. I went around trying to find more to hack at, like a little boy does with a new stick he has found in the woods. I felt someone watching me, looked up, and saw Joshua no longer welding his sword from side to side but resting upon it, his elbow on the hilt, the tip planted in the dirt, and watching me with a fond smile on his face.

"Having fun?" He said.

"Yes" I said, as I felt my face flush with a slight shade of red.

"Good. That is my *modus operandi*." He said, then smiled brightly.

"I have noticed." I said as I smiled back.

We had cleared the "wall" of sorts, and surprisingly not far behind that, Joshua pointed out a very narrow path that was almost hidden from view by a few small tuffs of grass that we had easily missed when we went ballistic on the greenery. These clumps of grass where situated directly in front of the start of the path and just enough to shield the path from view. Joshua had pulled the grass aside to reveal a small foot path that was no wider than five inches across. It reminded me of the kind of path one looks for in the forest when they are hunting small game; a dead giveaway that you have found an animal's daily foot path, and a good place to set up a snare so that later in the day you will have something to roast over a fire and fill the stomach with.

"What is that?" I asked.

"It is the path. We must follow it to find The Lands of Oblivion."

And with that, Joshua turned and began walking down the path, away from The City. I fell in step behind Him, unsure what He meant by "The Lands of Oblivion", but try as I might, unable not to feel a bit of a chill coarse through my body at the mentioning of its name. Something about that place, though I was totally uniformed about it, was unlike The Abode.

And as I suspected, almost immediately I began to learn how incredibly different The Lands of Oblivion were than the places I had been residing in. The moment I got on the path, I felt a distinct change in temperature. Instead of constant warmth I felt something like cold fog slide up against my skin. I suddenly wanted clothes for the warmth they brought and the way they sheltered me from the elements, and realized that I had forgotten of the carnal and basic purpose of clothes, for though one used them in the Countries of Matrimony to accentuate their overall glory and beauty, here on this path their use was in complete contrast.

Joshua looked over me, and seeing the way my skin had formed thousands of tiny bumps because of the cold, simply said, "Fire". Like someone had built a bonfire in my stomach, heat boiled up inside me from deep down within, and soon my skin was encased in an unseen source of warmth that left me without need of a blanket or sweater. The fog around me, now so thick, was repelled as though it was sickened by the heat that radiated from me, and when something unseen overhead did accumulate enough condensation from the air to form a droplet and drip it down upon me, shortly after making contact with my skin it steamed away again in its initial gaseous form.

The fog became thick, and we walked as though we were headed directly into it. The further in that we went, the darker it got around us. Soon we were in total blackness. I am not sure when I realized it, but I quickly noticed that all the fog was gone, and now we were in clear blackness, as dark as obsidian, as though someone had spilled ink over everything. I couldn't see anything around us, and it felt like the place was *blank*, apart from the path that our feet slowly pattered upon.

The "sky" (as we would have called it in past lives), or the infinite ceiling of the place we were in had shifted and become something disparate from what it was in the Countries. It had gone from magnificent colors to a dark, unlit black, looking much like a night sky on earth, but without any stars. In fact, there were no signs of even the least bit of light coming down from above. A lit match five miles above us would have cast more light upon the landscape than what the sky produced. Everything around us had changed so quickly, and I was slightly put on edge over it. Thankfully, Joshua and I were slightly glowing, as though the light from the Countries of Matrimony had left a residue upon us that wouldn't lift. The path itself would have been near to impossible to follow if it wasn't for this glow. I imagined a person without this inherent glow trying to follow the meager trail that we were traversing, and realized that the only way someone could manage would be to get down on their knees and literally crawl along, feeling the worn trail with their hands. If they didn't, undoubtedly within mere moments they would be lost, unable to find their way. I could clearly see Joshua in front me, but even then, what with the wild twists and turns that He was making in order to stay on the narrow way, I had difficultly staying on the path. There were points where innumerable paths branched out and sprouted from our own, less worn but nonetheless clearly cut into the ground, giving the one walking a dishonest verdict that it was the correct way. A few times for a brief moment I looked down at my feet, tired of tripping on the sides of the trail and hoping to see well enough to go without stumbling for a few minutes. That turned out to be a costly mistake, and I learned that keeping my eyes locked on Joshua and following Him, though I didn't know exactly where we were going which sometimes caused me to be tripped up and stutter along, was better than looking away and trying to do it on my own even though it seemed to be a bit more smooth of a ride when I looked down. The moment I looked away I lost sight of Joshua and immediately took the wrong path, suddenly encased in darkness except my own glow, which was significantly less bright when Joshua wasn't near me. When this happened I began to shout for Joshua, letting Him know that I wasn't behind Him anymore. The most eerie feeling came over me when I yelled the first time because I realized that the darkness was so thick that effortlessly swallowed up my words and Joshua was likely not hearing my desperate attempts to communicate with Him. A few times after yelling into the coal-black atmosphere and hearing my words bounce back to me like they had hit a resolute wall of soundlessness, effectively muffling my hollers, I admit that I acted like a child that thinks they have been left at the store by their parent when in fact the parent is simply on the isle next to their own, fully aware of the child's location. Joshua strode into view with a smile on His face, obviously able to hear my voice after all, despite the darkness' ability to consume my words and spit them back out completely suppressed and silenced. This happened a few times; losing my way and Him backtracking to find me, each time without reprimand but instead a smile and outstretched hand. I suppose He could have told me to keep a better eye on Him or to walk faster, but He never did. He seemed to take full responsibility for my well being. After a while I realized it was more effective, and more enjoyable, to simply hold His hand or keep my palm laid on His shoulder, letting touch guide me rather than sight. He didn't object.

After a very long time of walking, Joshua spoke. It felt as though we had been walking forever.

"I suspect you have a few questions for me, which would be understandable." I tripped on a mound of dirt in the middle of the path, steading myself on Joshua's shoulder.

"Yeah, you could say that." I said, though I didn't have the pressing need to have everything explained, like I had at different times previously. Something had settled in me, and I was not as concerned about what I was doing but who I was doing it with. I was happy just walking this path because I was walking it with Joshua, albeit it a dark one. I reasoned that one can live every moment looking forward to the next rather than enjoying the one they are in, thusly significantly diluting their entire existence and overall contentedness. Joy is found in the *now*, despite what the now holds. Hope is an altogether blessed thing, but cannot replace what is already present. I had learned that true happiness was found in what I already possessed but sometimes ceased to be aware of rather than the good things that were to come. All I needed was to be near Joshua, even though we were headed into a place that I assumed by our surroundings to be chilling, and I was content.

"You already know where we are going, but I am sure the nature of this path brings a few more questions to mind."

"Yes. Well, I guess I would ask, if The Eternal loves everyone, those back there," I pointed behind me, "*and*, as You say, those in the place we are headed, then that would mean that He wants the people we are about to visit to be living with Him in the Abode. Correct?"

"Yes. Of course."

"And if there are no walls around The City, then that means that You aren't keeping anyone out. Correct?" I said, slightly raising one of my eyebrows, as though I was saying something potentially risky.

"Very observant, Scythe. You are catching on." Joshua said. As we turned sharply to the left I caught a brief glance over His shoulder of His face looking satisfied and pleased.

There were logical implications to what Joshua had just agreed to, so I continued on. "And if there is a path between The Lands of Oblivion and The Countries of Matrimony, then I can't help but assume that people aren't only able to go from The Abode to The Lands of Oblivion, but also from The Lands of Oblivion to The Abode. Correct?"

"Yes. In part."

"In part?" I asked.

"Yes, in part. That will be explained more later. But what you are really asking is if The Eternal keeps people in The Lands of Oblivion, making this path a one way street, or if this path can run both ways."

I thought for a moment. "Yes, I suppose that is at the heart of what I am asking."

"Then yes, it runs both ways. The Eternal would never keep someone somewhere, anywhere, against their desire, both The Lands of Oblivion *or* The Countries of Matrimony."

I ignored this last statement, feeling it was too much to grasp at the moment, for I was barely able to grasp the most simple of facts that we were trying to tack down, and was using all of my mental capacity just to accomplish that. I continued on.

"So, if the passage is open to men to go from The Lands of Oblivion to the Abode...." I said with a sense of finality, "...then this is my main question; Since anyone is welcome in the Countries of Matrimony, why would The Eternal make the path so incredibly hard to follow in order to get there?"

"Brilliant question! Now we are getting somewhere. In short, The Eternal never made the path hard to follow, or made it at all. Men did."

"What do you mean?" I said, as we rounded a tight corner in the trail to the left, Joshua facing away from me, His eyes focused on the trail. Joshua stopped walking and turned around so that we were face to face, as though He didn't want me to miss what He was about to say.

"Well, understand that everything and everyone first started in The Countries of Matrimony. Men did not begin outside the Presence of The Eternal but began within It from the onset. For various reasons, reasons we shall soon hear from the inhabitants of the territories, some fled from the goodness of The Eternal. Men desired to distance themselves from Him and..."

I couldn't help but interrupt. "But why would they ever want to be distanced from Him? He was..." my voice trailed off while my brain attempted to search its recesses for a word that accurately described Him, even just to describe Him in part, but it couldn't, so I gave a shot at a description instead, which was pathetically less than a fraction of what I wanted to sum up; "...nothing short of every desire in my heart, fulfilled."

"Well said, Scythe. *That* is the question of the ages. The greatest mystery is not really why bad things happen to good people or if The Eternal allows suffering, but why men ever wanted anything but The Eternal in the first place, and why they made their way away from Him when He was nothing but perfect towards them. Why they would choose a tree that bore the fruits of the knowledge of *evil* over unconditional *life* is quite a conundrum. Or how about why they would want a man to speak to The Eternal for them rather than speak to Him themselves? Why they would reject His goodness and cower in fear from His gentleness is *the* mystery of mysteries, and one that is without an answer that is satisfactory.

But as I was saying, men desired to distance themselves from The Eternal, and when they did, they made this pathetic path away from Him."

Joshua's words were not settling into my mind as I hoped, so I blurted out a more simplified version of my question,

"Why does Heaven set itself so far from hell if The Eternal loves those that are there?"

"Heaven did not put itself far from hell. Hell put itself far from heaven. History always reveals The Eternal's persistent pursuit of man and man's persistent fleeing from His love."

"Wait..." I said, remembering Joshua's words from a few moments before, "....did you say men made this path?"

"Yes. This path is the combined efforts of men to distance themselves from the affection of The Father.

Love was too wonderfully uncomfortable for them. In hopes to deter anyone coming after them that would hunt them down with grace and lure them back to the sheer pleasure and bliss of My Presence, they pioneered into this darkness, blindly weaving back and forth hoping to throw off anyone following them."

"And that is why the entrance to the trail was overgrown! They tried to disguise it from us so that we didn't come after them!" I exclaimed.

"Exactly. Very good Scythe. Their shame and guilt creeps up and covers the only entrance to their world, trying to seal it off from our attempts to remind them of their destiny and draw them back into The Abode. That is why it is so enjoyable to violently hack at the growth that tries to camouflage this path. I have never been one that got along very well with shame and guilt."

Joshua turned and continued walking, keeping a brisk pace as though He didn't want to linger upon the path. I held His hand and followed behind in the wake of His glow.

"So they choose this place. Fully." I said, unable to hold back a bit of sadness in my voice but nonetheless with a frankness.

"Yep." Joshua said, matter of factly.

"What if they change their mind and want to go back?"

"Nobody is stopping them. But that is when their choices to disguise the path and hide from grace catch up to them. They have done such a thorough job at making the path impossible to follow that when they want to backtrack and make their way out they can't find their way. The whole problem with finding the Abode on their own is that the entrance is so overgrown and narrow when you get close that one can spend thousands of years just a few feet from its entrance and they will still never find it. And that is if they make it that far into the darkness, which few do. *None* have ever found their way on their own. And many have tried. After enough fruitless expeditions they get offended, discouraged, or bored, and eventually make their way back to The Lands of Oblivion."

"Why don't you just straighten the path, widen it, and turn on the lights to make it easy for them to find the way?" I said.

"They *want* it like this. We won't override their will. If we win them over by force, then we never really won them at all. We are confident that we can play by their rules and still win the match. This insures that we really do win their hearts fully. It wouldn't be hard to just program them to love us by removing their desires, but when we remove the ability to choose darkness we also remove their ability to choose love that is real and genuine. And love, a true relational connection based on trust and intimacy, is our main goal. Even if it takes hundreds of thousands of years, we will succeed. My Father and I can be very persistent."

"Well, if they cannot find their way to the Abode, what are their hopes for ever getting out?"

"On their own? Oh, none. They will never make it to the Abode unless I help them find the way. There is no hope for those that try to go it alone. That is why I make these trips. If they follow Me I will show them the way. And that is what we are going to do. We are going help those that want to come back home."

"I pieced that much together." I said as I smiled, though Joshua couldn't see my face as I was still walking behind Him.

"So," I continued, "Since men get lost trying to make their way to the Abode, do men ever get lost when they leave the Abode and head into The Lands of Oblivion?"

"Yes, but they eventually find their way because the path gets wider the closer they come to The Lands of Oblivion. As long as someone continues into the darkness, it will funnel them into The Lands of Oblivion."

"And have others accompanied You on these assignments as I am?"

"Some. But most of the time the Matchmaker prepares them and I go alone and get them."

"The Matchmaker?"

"Yes. Just as He was before, He is still preparing the hearts of men." Joshua said.

"And does it work?"

"We have managed to woo many back to the light, but upon meeting Me, some leave The Lands of Oblivion and continue on into the blackness, going even deeper and further away, hoping that they won't have to see Me again and listen to Me remind them who they are." Joshua said over His shoulder.

I imagined that the rejection Joshua must feel on these trips would be paralyzing, but He seemed completely unaffected as He spoke about it. Nonetheless, not wanting to bring up a sensitive topic I asked, "You mentioned 'the blackness'. What is that?"

"Some that fled from the Abode went further than others. The Abyss is what lies beyond The Lands of Oblivion. And beyond that, The Burning Guilt. On this trip we are going to visit the *people* that went the shortest distance and depth away from the light."

And as Joshua finished speaking, I saw over His shoulder something in the darkness looming up in front of us. It was a building, dark like a shadow, rectangular and standing up but tilted, as though its foundation had been rattled by an earthquake and it now stood with a limp like a wounded animal. It had one small window, dust and cobwebs hanging from it, no decorations or texture, and appeared to be as bland as a thing can get. It was disheartening just looking at it.

"Are we....there yet?"

"Yes." Joshua said. "This is The Lands of Oblivion. Pathetic, isn't it?"

Eleven

.

I was astounded that anyone would want to live in the place I was beholding with my eyes. It wasn't just that the air felt stale the way a small room does when the windows and door have been locked shut for days, but there was no color, no sound, and no feeling. There wasn't any stimulation of any sort. One couldn't see into the distance and find mountains on the horizon because the darkness hampered one's ability to see further than twenty or so feet, and even if I had been able to see into the distance, I doubt that something as majestic as mountains would have been there anyways. The light that was there (if one could call it light) felt fake and electric, deeply gray and yellow, even heavy and thick rather than weightless and clear, somewhat more like smoke than light at all. It felt as though at any moment we would be plunged into the darkest of darkness because the battery or other makeshift source of power that was behind the weak shadowlight was destined to fail us in a matter of time.

A campsite set up by ten year olds would have been more inspiring than this feeble attempt at a *place*. It was the epitome of drab, which quickly would have become boredom, disillusionment, and apathy of the greatest proportions if I hadn't had the glow of Joshua standing beside me. This place was joyless. I couldn't help but think how incredibly stupid a person must be for choosing to live in a place like this, especially when they had a mansion in the Abode to live in. I wasn't sure if I would ever be able to understand someone's choice of living here. I knew I would never agree, but I was very curious to hear and understand their reasoning, as it was evidently powerful enough to keep them here.

Just then, someone came bustling through the door on the side of the tilted building and said loudly, "Greetings! Greetings! Welcome! Welcome!"

The overweight man waddling towards us was dressed in a way that disturbed me, and his exuberance felt exactly like his clothes; fake. On his head sat a gold crown with big precious stones set into it that were meant to look like the real thing but were clearly made of plastic. It was overstated and gaudy. The gold on the crown wasn't gold at all but just paint, as most of it had fallen off and what was left was in the process of peeling away. He wore a large robe, but it didn't flow out behind him as he made his way towards us but rather just hung at his side as though it was a dead animal. It had holes in it and had obviously been stepped on many times or dragged through the dirt; the part that should hang near the ground wasn't properly measured so it drug across the ground as he walked. As he got closer I realized that it was not a real robe at all, but something most people have hung up in their bathroom or beside their bed for cover during midnight trips to the sink for a glass of water. He had obviously mistaken this robe for something it wasn't. His boots, his pants and shirt, all of it, were a counterfeit of the real thing. It all gave me an eerie feeling.

I looked at the man then at Joshua, bewildered. Joshua was smiling, but the sort of smile one wears when they have met someone many times before and are about to go through the same meaningless presentation as last time, like a door to door salesman that shows up every week but that you never buy anything from. It seems this man wasn't getting the point. And we hadn't even said anything yet.

"I am most flattered at thy presence!" the man squealed.

"Hello Ethelwulf" Joshua said passively, as He exhaled.

"Yes, yes, yes. Hello Joshua." Ethelwulf said dismissively, as he waved his hand at Joshua. "But who is this fine gentleman that you have brought to be my guest?" He cooed with a high, shrill voice. He spoke in a way that seemed to be an attempt at a dignified quality, rolling his "r"s and causing his voice to climb and plummet in tone to accentuate his points, but fitting right in with the rest of his appearance, it came across as a failed attempt at something he was not.

"This," Joshua waved towards me, "is Scythe. We have come to visit you."

"Oh I am sure you have, dear sir!" Ethelwulf said sarcastically. "You going to take this one from under the roof of my protection and provision as well?" Ethelwulf sneered.

"Yes. Just like the other times, we aren't here to stay." Joshua said gently, like he was talking to someone gone through incredible loss or tragedy that called for incredible sensitively. "I am sorry to disappoint you."

"I am *quite* used to it by now, my *friend*." Ethelwulf shot back, then his face was wiped clean, into a plastic smile as he turned to me. "Welcome to my kingdom. Please come in and make yourself at home in my castle."

I looked around for the castle he was speaking of. Ethelwulf must have known that I didn't recognize his house to be the "castle" he was speaking of, and frowned disapprovingly when I looked around curiously.

"This way!" he shouted, then quickly shook his head into a unnatural smile, correcting his outburst.

We followed Ethelwulf into his house, and he began rummaging around in a cabinet, looking for a tea set that seemed to be distributed in different spots in his colorless kitchen.

Ethelwulf's house showed signs of being erected by someone who had never built a house before. It looked to have started out as one room, then everything had been built on from that first room as time went on. It was more of a large add-on than a badly constructed house. Some rooms could only be accessed by walking through other rooms, as the place lacked a hallway, a characteristic in a home that I was now realizing signifies an actual *plan* before construction began. There were no straight walls or ninety-degree corners. Everything was makeshift and disordered. There was a thick layer of dust on everything, so much so that things were barely discernible, such as the portraits on the walls of people dressed as kings and queens on earth.

I was somewhat surprised, and surprisingly disturbed, at a few of the pictures that hung on the wall. They were framed in wood that had been coated by the same tasteless gold paint, again peeling away, and depicted none other than Joshua Himself. They weren't photographs, but painted depictions of Him. One showed Joshua with a dove coming down upon Him as light surrounded Him, another with Him holding a lamb in His arms as He spoke to a group of people. Oddly enough, though I thoroughly loved Joshua, these pictures gave me the same feeling that Ethelwulf's crown did. They felt as though they were without life, artificial, and lacking any sense of real beauty. They hung there on the dusty wall without genuine creativity and deficient of the most remote sense of artistic taste.

"These are pictures of Joshua. Why do *you* have them?" The words slipped out of my mouth without my consent.

"Whatever do you mean, my dear boy? I am not just a great king, but a highly religious man!" Ethelwulf bellowed in a bragging tone.

"Yes, but..." I thought for a moment, trying to think of how to say what I wanted to say without offending the mock king, "what use is a picture when the real thing is standing before you?"

"Him?" Ethelwulf cackled, clearly amused at my question and pointing at Joshua in disbelief, his large stomach jiggling up and down, waves of fat rippling back and forth from the vibrations of his laughter.

"Yes!" I said adamantly.

"Ah, he is a fine fellow I suppose, but not like *Him!*" He gestured towards the dust covered pictures.

I looked at Joshua and he looked back, quickly molding His face into a cheesy smile that bared His teeth in a overzealous fashion like a mother had just asked him to smile for a family picture that he wasn't ready for so he wore the first conjured up face he could think of. It was a hilarious smile, and immediately broke the intensity of the moment. I couldn't help but laugh. It was as though Joshua wasn't bothered in the least bit at Ethelwulf's ignorance and dishonor towards Him.

"Is that right?" I said, turning my attention back to Ethelwulf and speaking as seriously as I could while attempting to suppress my laughter. Something unspoken had occurred to me and I now felt like I was talking to a child and wanted to be tender with Ethelwulf. He was obviously a confused man. My tone was understanding and calm, yet confident.

"Yes it is." the fat man said matter-of-factly, almost defiantly.

"Well, we didn't come to debate if I am like the man in the pictures or not, my friend." Joshua said disarmingly. "We have come to see if you would like to leave your kingdom for Mine."

"Why would I ever leave this place?" Ethelwulf said more declaring than asking. "I have built it up to such extravagance that to leave it would be a great waste! Can't you understand this?"

"I understand perfectly." Joshua said tenderly, as though He really did understand. "Perhaps you could just take a vacation from your work here? We would love to host you in my land for as long, or as short, of a time as you please."

"Ah! Trying to out-serve me, are you?" He said defensively. "You are here in my house, under my roof and in my care and all you can talk about is yourself! Just let me show you how I do hospitality, and I am sure you won't want to leave!"

Then he whispered, "It gets so frightfully lonely here." I am quite sure he meant to say it under his breath and only to himself, but Joshua and I both clearly heard him.

Ethelwulf moved sluggishly around the room, finally rounding up three tea cups, then passed them out with a proud look on his face, as though he had just accomplished some great feat. I was surprised to see that there was no tea in my cup, not even water. It was empty.

"But where is the tea?" I said.

Joshua lowered His head, obviously hiding His face from view so that Ethelwulf wouldn't mistaken His laughter at my statement to be Him laughing at the lack of tea.

"Do you see any water around here, boy? Ethelwulf snapped bitterly. "Let alone, tea?"

"Of course. I'm sorry. The cups are...wonderful. Thank you." I said.

"That is much better." Ethelwulf said with an air of superiority. "You must learn gratefulness my friend. It is deemed highly in the scriptures."

"Very true, very true." I said agreeably. It was easier to just concur with this man than to engage every mistaken point he made.

"Please come with us, Ethelwulf." Joshua said, pleadingly, but with a bluntness that caused Ethelwulf to look Joshua directly in the eyes.

"I cannot. Without my reign, my lands will fall into ruin. I have *responsibility* here, Joshua, something you obviously know very little about."

"You have created responsibilities for yourself so that boredom didn't drive you completely mad. But these responsibilities were never yours to begin with. You only have responsibly within the realms of authority that my Father gives, and your authority does not exist in this land."

"That is enough!" Ethelwulf barked abruptly.

Joshua continued in a near whisper, undeterred by Ethelwulf's little explosion. "But that is not all." Ethelwulf looked up from his pathetic tea cup that he had been staring into with shame because of his verbal outburst. "You are a king. Just not here. You must come with me to have the desires of your heart fulfilled. You must have the humility to let me give to you without you trying to conjure something up on your own."

"Joshua, I *am* humble. I just like to serve more than to receive. That is what *He* did anyways." He gestured to the paintings again. "You would know that if you knew the scriptures at all. A true leader is determined by his ability to serve others."

"That is true. But one must first receive from Me before they have any ability to serve. You can only give away what you have been given. Let me give my lands to you. Come with Me, please. I miss your presence. I want to be near you."

I was watching them talk, my head looking at one, then turning to look at the other. They had obviously been through this before.

"If you want to be with me so badly, you should stay with me here." Ethelwulf said. I have to admit I thought this was quite a good comeback.

"Ethelwulf, I would stay here for millions of years if that is what it took to have you come with Me. But I have visited you regularly and you have never enjoyed it when I come. This is because this place isn't healthy for you. The only place where you will remember who you are is in the Abode. That place will have an effect on your mind that you have forgotten. If I were to stay here with you, you would eventually flee once again, and go even further into the recesses of this place. You are not ready for the kind of love that I would give you if I stayed here."

"You are right about that!" Ethelwulf snorted. "Perhaps you could come back another time then, my friend. Thank you for your visit. It is high time for me to take a nap."

Joshua ignored his dismissal. "Ethelwulf, if you truly want to be a king, follow Me."

"I am already a king. Can't you see?" And he waved his hand slowly out in front of himself with his palm up, as though he was showing someone a table with the finest of foods displayed across it.

"Yes. I can." Joshua said sadly. He let out a long exhale then said, "Lets excuse ourselves, Scythe."

I stood, awkwardly handed back the empty tea cup to Ethelwulf, and turned to go.

"Please come back. Even if it is the two of you; I do enjoy the company" Ethelwulf called out. Then he whispered too loudly again, "It does get frightfully lonely here."

My heart broke. Despite how confused, dirty, proud, and dislikable Ethelwulf was, I still felt sad for him in his loneliness.

"So he is just going to stay here?" I asked as I thought of actually living in this place, especially falling asleep alone in such a dark and looming place. It gave me the chills.

"Yes." Joshua said quietly, as though it grieved Him as much as it did me. We had started walking around the side of Ethelwulf's house, away from the direction where the Abode's entrance was located.

"How many times have you gone and seen him?" I asked.

"Numerous."

"And he has always been this way?"

"Yes. But that is not who he really is." Joshua said, with an interesting longing in His voice.

"What do you mean?" I asked.

"Ethelwulf *is* a man of great royalty, there is no question about that. But everything that a person is can only really come to the surface in its fullness when that person has given all that they are to Me. Ethelwulf believes that because he is a king it is beneath him to submit to anyone else. You can see the logic behind it. But the greatest of kings are the ones that have given themselves to be a servant to *the* King. Nonetheless, some reason that it is better to be a king in hell than a servant in heaven. This is what Ethelwulf believes in his heart. He does not know that the most lowly servant there," and He pointed back towards the narrow entrance to the Abode, "is incomparably more powerful and glorious than the most high king here."

As he said this, we were getting further and further from Ethelwulf's house. I couldn't help but think if our interaction with him was his last chance to come to the Abode.

"So is that it for him? Is that the last time You will extend an invitation to Ethelwulf to come with You to The Countries of Matrimony?"

Joshua looked at me with surprise. "No Scythe. Never. I will keep coming until Ethelwulf allows Me to love him. I started a good work in him, just as I did you, and I will be faithful to complete it. If I didn't finish what I started, I would be unfaithful, and unfaithfulness is something I am incapable of. You do know that there are certain things I *can't* do, right?"

I smiled and nodded as a feeling in my heart burst to life anew at being reminded of who He was; It was so easy to forget. His words made my heart bloom to life over and over again, unfolding to the light of His being. I had to admit that my affection for Him had not plained out, though I had spent considerable time with Him. Affection only grew.

I spoke. "Yes. You cannot do what isn't in accordance with Your nature."

"Well said." He said.

And with that, we left Ethelwulf far behind us, sipping on his imaginary tea in his ramshackle house, wearing his feigned clothes of forgery.

Twelve

"It doesn't feel necessarily *evil* here. Just empty, which, don't get me wrong, is incredibly despairing. But I guess I expected something different." I said. I had been thinking about it since we had been on the narrow path.

"Very observant of you. Hell isn't so much the presence of evil as much as it is the absence of The Eternal. Evil takes shape only outside the presence of light. All one has to do to live in hell is to step away from light and willingly shut the door to it. This place was a place of intentional exclusion of the Eternal."

"I wouldn't have believed it before, but now I can see how that is true. Its odd," I paused, checking myself again, "But though I can sense this is a hollow place, I don't feel that way. This atmosphere isn't affecting me on the inside like I assume it should." I said.

"That is because you are with Me. If you were here alone, the walls of darkness would fall down upon you and you would feel the oppression of the absence of light and life. Terror reigns here."

"Absence of life?" I asked. "But Ethelwulf was obviously alive."

"True." Joshua said plainly. "But since the Eternal is the source to all life, and because the inhabitants of this land have attempted to be removed from Him, the result is that they die over and over again, even dying moment by moment. But death here is not as it was in the past life. Here death is not an event, but a constant reality. Their death never lets them leave this place. It is relentless, persistent, unyielding, and unending. Even their living is death. And," Joshua sighed as though there was much more to divulge that He did not enjoy, "time is unending here. Everything moves at a crawling rate. It is as though everyone is constantly waiting for something of the utmost imperative to be brought about, but it just is never executed. It isn't much different than the way one used to feel when they are standing in a long checkout line at the store on Christmas Eve, trying to get some last minute presents. All they want to do is get home, but the line doesn't seem to be moving so they wait and wait and wait. They are able to just drop the worthless object in their hands and in return spend their time in a much more meaningful way with their family on such a special evening, but they don't. They are able to leave but convinced they must stay. The waiting one does here isn't much different, though more severe. Their waiting never ends unless..."

"...unless they come with You. Right?" I couldn't help but finish His thought.

"Yes." Joshua smiled proudly. I loved that it wasn't hard to make Him proud of me.

"We are headed this way." Joshua pointed into the inky blackness, as though He knew right where we were going, though I couldn't see anything and it looked like Joshua was pointing directly into the surface of a blackboard rather than into the distance.

I followed, and soon we were walking up to another building of sorts. We had only walked for a few minutes and down a gentle incline from Ethelwulf's house, but something about the air felt like we were pushing through and against something thick, thus made walking short distances seem to take longer and sapped more energy than a walk in the Abode or on earth. I couldn't help but feel that even the air deemed us uninvited in this place and did its best at holding us at bay. This didn't matter to me. If I was with Joshua, it didn't matter who hadn't invited us. Authority is sustained by motive, and our motive was as pure as something can get. I had confidence about our being there.

We approached a door that seemed to made of broken and pockmarked wood, nestled in the wall of another misshapen and haphazard excuse of a building. I remembered that orphans have been known to call garbage dumps home, and that knowing who we are and what we deem to be home has everything to do with who we belong to. If we do not know who awaits our return we bed anywhere we find warmth, even if it be alongside pigs and amidst their waste. It was clear from the state of this "home" that the person on the other side of this door knew not whose child they were.

Joshua knocked firmly on the door. The latch must not have been fully set, because His rapping caused the the door to come ajar and swing open enough for us to see inside. Rather than our last stop that carried a facade of royalty, this place had no "theme", unless complete disorder can be considered a theme. Things were sprawled all over the floor, mold seemed to grow on most if not all of the items spread about, and there were piles and piles of worthless objects. It was as though we had just walked into the nest of a pack rat.

The door had only swung open enough for us to be able to peek in, so Joshua placed His hand on the door and started to push the door, but soon was deterred as the door stopped moving, like someone was on the other side, keeping it from being opened further. Joshua lowered His head and put His shoulders into it, obviously using some of His physical strength to push with more force. The door started to budge, and as I heard crashes and scraping sounds I realized that it wasn't any person that was keeping us out, but the piles of debris were in the door's path.

As we stepped inside it as was though we hit another wall, but this one was unseen and possibly more deterring than the stuck door. This wall was the invisible stench that hung in the air, most likely caused by the mold and bottled up air, as there were no windows to leave opened, and the door had obviously not been opened for quite some time. "Stale" didn't do it justice. This air had been re-breathed so many times it no longer possessed any ability to give life to one's lungs.

I looked around as I coughed and saw small mountains of specific items. On my left, a hill of used plastic gloves. On my right, a three-foot tall pile of dentures. There was a unsettling feeling about the place, as though the person had never learned that some things should be discarded to the trash because they had absolutely no worth. Even if, for some odd reason, they had an attachment to these items, any rational person could come to the conclusion that simply for the reason of health it would be best to get rid of this stuff. The environment this garbage created was uninhabitable.

That is when I saw it, or should I say, her. Something moved, buried within in a pile on my far right by the wall. Something gray and discolored, even slightly green, came into focus and I recognized it to be a slim, boney arm.

Joshua saw it too, and before I could react, He had leapt over the heaps of trash towards the engulfed body. Like a man that just found the X on the map that marks the spot to a buried treasure, He fell to His knees and began wildly whipping away the various plastic bags, moldy clothes, and other objects that were covering the person.

Finally He removed the last plastic bag, which was positioned directly across the woman's face, and as it came away she gasped for air as though her head had been forced underwater for minutes and only now had she resurfaced. Her chest rose and fell with great speed, and her widened eyes darting about the room communicated complete terror. Joshua grabbed her hand and began to repeat over and over in a voice that was nearly silent and of the utmost tenderness, "I am here. You are ok. I am with you. You will be ok."

Her face slowly adjusted from dread to normalcy as she locked eyes with Joshua and sapped off of the strength in His eyes. I saw her hand grip His after a few moments, as though she accepted his comfort and was asking for it not to cease.

Joshua looked at me. "She was suffocating. I am glad we came when we did."

I didn't know why it mattered if we had come now or later, as death didn't claim someone from this place to take them somewhere else like it did on earth, but I didn't say anything. It wasn't the time to ask questions.

Joshua spoke as though He knew what I was asking. "She was asleep. The sounds of opening the door must have awakened her, and she sucked the bag into her mouth. The weight of the garbage piled on her kept her from being able to knock it away. It doesn't matter that she wouldn't have died from suffocation, but that she *felt* that she would have. I am concerned with how she feels, and want her to have peace, despite if reality lines up with how she feels or not."

I simply nodded back in understanding. Then it occurred to me that I hadn't slept since I arrived in The Abode, which made measuring my time since that point hard to quantify. What was more puzzling was *why* I hadn't needed to sleep. A question for another time, unless of course Joshua answers it without me asking again. I waited, but He didn't speak, so I resolved myself to ask Him later.

"He said you would be coming." The woman said horsely as she coughed up some phlegm and spit it onto the floor a few feet away. I gagged. Joshua did not.

"Yes. He did." Joshua replied gently, slightly pulling His head back and cocking it to the side as He smiled, like He was standing back to observe some beautiful piece of art.

"He said you would make me well. Is this really true? Doctors told me that my whole life, but it never amounted to much more than me losing every penny."

"The Matchmaker was correct. I can make you well. In fact..." Joshua turned to me and waved me over, "...here is Scythe. He has a gift for you from the lands I dwell in. Scythe, please give her the leaves."

I had almost forgotten about the leaves in my pants. I reached into my right pocket and pulled out the crumpled, bright leaves, holding them outstretched in my hand before her. The leaves shed more light in the room than any of the sources of dwindling light the woman had in the house. Aside from Joshua, they were the brightest thing there, and their color reminded me that this realm of gray wasn't the reality of every place. I thought back to the wildness of the colors in The Abode and The Spectrum and felt a rush of peace surged through me.

The woman reached out and took the leaves, looking at them closely and holding them up inquisitively to her face. Her skin was not pink but had a green and gray sheen, and not because of the light coming from the leaves. She was clearly ill, and had been that way for a very long time.

"Eat them." Joshua said.

"How do I know you aren't here to poison me?" She said.

"You don't."

"Ah! Whats to lose?" She said heedlessly, and shoved the leaves into her mouth. As she chewed, a look of absolute delight spread across her face. It was the first time I had seen someone other than Joshua genuinely smile in a while.

"They are delicious!" She exclaimed.

"Yes. Everything is in The Countries of Matrimony."

"Lands of Matrimony? I could get used to that. Who is being married?" She asked.

"You." Joshua said.

The woman laughed heartily. "Excuse me? Me? Getting married? Who would have me? Look at me!"

She stood and modeled her boney body for us, then a look of surprise ambushed her face suddenly.

"I haven't gotten out of bed for as long as I can remember! All I could do was sleep. Those leaves really did the trick!"

"I would have you." Joshua said.

"What?" The woman asked, as though she hadn't heard Him correctly.

"I would marry you." Joshua said in a sincere and serious voice.

"I don't understand...." She said as her voice trailed off. I thought that for a second, amidst the gray and jade shiny hue of her skin, I caught sight of a bit of red flush her cheeks.

"I think you do." Joshua replied. "The Matchmaker told you everything you need to know about Me. He told you that I am in love with you, and that I always have been. He told you that I would heal you, care for you, and cherish you. Did He not?"

"He did. But it was too good to be true."

"Well, now you know He was right. Will you have me?" Joshua said, as He extended His hand to her in invitation.

The woman suddenly looked bewildered and uncomfortable. "Will I have you? Are you kidding? Will you have me! Of course I would receive You! But do you not see the woman in front of you? Do you not understand who you would be forever joined to?"

"I do. I see you as you really are. You do not." Joshua said.

"Buddy, I know who I am. I know what I have done, and I know what this body looks like when there aren't any rags hanging off it. No man wants *this*." She gestured to her body in a sweeping motion, encompassing all of her.

"You are mistaken. You *are* beautiful. You are wanted. And in order for that to become true to all, it must become true to you first. But that can only happen if your opinion of yourself is determined by what I think rather than what you think."

We sat there in silence for a minute or two as she took Joshua's words in. Then suddenly, her arm shot out and grabbed Joshua's hand as though she thought He may change His mind.

"Valerie. That is my name." She said quietly, almost shyly, with her face looking at the ground as she held His hand.

"Valerie, it is very nice to meet you. Would it be too much for you to model yourself for us again?"

I was shocked that Joshua asked her to do this, as the first time through she modeled her body in a distasteful, seductive way. The first time was disturbing not just because the way she moved suggested to overt sexuality, but because her body wasn't the modeling type and wouldn't have caused the most desperate of men to desire her.

But surprisingly, Valerie stood to do as Joshua requested, but right before she began making seductive movements, she looked down at her body that was covered by a shirt and shorts and gasped. Her skin had cleared up. The greenish sheen that had made her skin look almost oiled down was now pink and full of color. Her bones had stopped sticking out from her skin, as though she had gained weight, enough to give her womanly curves, but not enough for her to feel that she needed to lose weight.

And as we watched her watching herself, the edges of her shirt and shorts began to unravel slightly. The loose ends of the fabric then started to extend and grow, then began to weave themselves back together, resulting in the garments completely transforming before our eyes from rags to riches. In a few moments she was covered in a strikingly white dress, shining like a lighthouse in the darkness.

"Oh my!" I exclaimed involuntarily. Joshua was right; She *was* beautiful. I hadn't the eyes to see it. The woman that now stood before me looked nothing like the woman from moments ago, but little details like the shape of her nose or the set height of her cheekbones told me that it was in fact her.

Her surprise at her own beauty did not cause her to forget the request that had been made by Joshua. She began to spin before Him, like a girl in a field of mustard flowers when she thinks nobody is looking. It was motion that communicated both play and thanksgiving. Her spin came to a dizzy stop, her giggling and falling into Joshua's arms like He had held her a thousand times before.

"I wanted to believe it was true." She said.

"Everything the Matchmaker told you was true. He did His job well. Come with me. Leave this place and cleave to Me." Joshua said, almost desperately, as though He wanted what He held in His arms more than anything else.

Her face dropped briefly. "I'm not sure I can leave all of this. This is what I am familiar with, though it may not be much. I don't do well with change."

"I understand. Could you leave all of this if you knew that there are far greater treasures waiting for you in My lands?"

"Well, it isn't that I doubt that what You have to offer is of more material worth and beauty than what I have here. Its that every little thing in here means something to me on a level of sentimental value."

"Ah, yes." Joshua said.

"Will you excuse me for a moment? I want to see my face in a mirror." Valerie asked.

"Of course." Joshua said, and Valerie walked out of the room and into a nearby bathroom, then closed the door.

Joshua turned to me. "Scythe, have you ever met someone that hoards things?"

"I have heard of it, but I have never seen it before. There wasn't enough of one thing on earth during my life there for anyone to be able to hoard it."

"Well," Joshua went on, "Someone that hoards things does so because of an uncommon and unhealthy connection with material things that is based on a need for love. Valerie saves these things because of a need for relational connection."

"That makes no sense to me." I said.

"I get that. Let me explain. Valerie's family abandoned her long ago because of some of her more odd characteristics. Relationships with her son and daughter deteriorated and eventually they hadn't spoken for many years when she was on earth. Try as she might, she wasn't able to bridge the relational gap that widened between her and her children. And so that she could feel as though she was still loved by them, she would buy things she liked, wrap them up as a gift, write on the package that it was from her daughter or son, and then on her birthday or Christmas morning she would unwrap it, convincing herself that her child had given the gift to her. She would then bond with that item in the same way and with the same strength that a mother loves her child. It was her only connection to those that she loved. This misplaced love and grief became more and more extreme, expanding to more than just gifts she would buy for herself, but to every material thing she came across. *Things* became her peace, and not even things that were of any value, just anything that *existed*. Some people are so starved for love that they feast on food of no sustenance. It isn't much different from the way a child bonds with a stuffed teddy bear...just sad rather than cute. The need for love can pervert someone's mind so greatly if it is not rightly satisfied."

Joshua paused and leaned forward to make sure that the door to the bathroom was still closed. Then He continued.

"Thus, what has become Valerie's comfort," and He pointed across the room, "has now become what she does not want to let go of. Her world will literally come apart if this trash is forcefully taken from her and thrown away. To throw all of this away without her consent would be like killing her children before her eyes. This has to be something *she* chooses. But she will only do that if the root issue, the need to feel loved and connected relationally, is met fully. That is what I am doing now."

He had left me speechless again. I didn't have any thoughts to add to the conversation because He had so thoroughly explained exactly what was going on.

Valerie came out of the bathroom a few moments later. It was clear that she had been crying.

"It isn't that I don't want to come. I do want to. It is just that...that..."

Joshua got up and went over to her, holding her in His arms.

"I know it is hard. Trust Me. I will never leave your side. Ever. You can be with Me forever. Will you leave this place for some place much more wonderful?"

Valerie looked around the room for a moment, and through tears began laughing, saying, "Can you believe this dump? What a hell hole! Yes! I will come. But the only way I can do it is if I just close my eyes and you carry me out. Otherwise I know that I will want to grab little things as I go, and if I start doing that then I am going to want to grab more, until there will be so much to carry that I will just stay."

Valerie closed her eyes, and Joshua picked her up in her white dress the way a groom carries a bride over the threshold. Joshua navigated through the piles of filth, carrying Valerie in his arms, and we made our way outside. Though the air in The Lands of Oblivion wasn't in the least bit desirable, it was better than the stale, moldy, disease ridden, air inside Valerie's house.

Joshua put Valerie down, and started walking in the direction of The Abode. As He passed me, He whispered ecstatically, "We got one!"

I laughed and asked, "Are we taking her back right now?"

"Of course! No time to wait! She has no idea what is awaiting her there."

Thirteen

Joshua led Valerie by the hand into the blackness towards the narrow path leading back to The Abode. I fell into place behind them and kept my eyes peeled on Valerie's back so as not to lose my way.

After a short stent of time, Valerie started to slow in speed, obviously becoming tired.

"Not in the best of shape I guess." She said.

Joshua stopped walking so as to give her a rest, and we stood in the shadows of that underworld.

"Take your time, Valerie." Joshua said.

"Thank you. I think all I need is a small nap." Valerie said as she yawned.

I watched as her eyelids drooped over her eyes and she let out a long, weary yawn, though it had been less than ten minutes that we had been walking. This concerned me somewhat, as we had only just begun on our journey.

"A nap may seem as though it would help," Joshua said, "But it won't really result in the energy you will need. You would need to sleep for years to get the energy you need for this walk, and if you slept that long, you would forget what we are doing and where we are going."

"Then what do I do? I can barely stay awake!" Valerie said through another drawn-out yawn.

"The closer you get to the light of The Abode the easier it will be to stay awake. I will help you. Focus on holding onto my hand. I will lead you." Joshua said.

Valerie put on a determined face and gripped Joshua's hand as we started walking again. I couldn't piece together why Valerie was so weak and needed sleep but I hadn't had any need for sleep since I had entered The Abode. As I always did, I asked Joshua when I couldn't make sense of something.

"You haven't needed to sleep because your skin took in the light of The Abode and the higher levels. She hasn't." He pointed to Valerie, who was still making her best effort to continue walking and not succumb to sleep.

"What do you mean?" I said.

"Man was never intended to sleep for the purpose of rest. Rest was a constant reality before the Fall, even in the context of work. It was *the* reality. Rest was not something anyone had to be intentional about; it was a ever-present fact that one couldn't help but experience because of the light."

"The light?" I asked.

"Yes. After the Fall, men's bodies stopped being able to take the light from The Eternal or the sun and convert it into energy, at least not to the degree they once could." Joshua said over His shoulder as He continued to follow the increasingly narrow path.

"Are you saying, I mean, the same way that plants do?" I asked, stumbling over my words.

"Yes. Photosynthesis wasn't something that just green foliage was able to do. Everything did it. My Father and I possess the light of life. Nothing slept, for they were energized not by the night but by the constant light of day. They didn't get more and more weak as time went on, but more and more strong. Years added to one's life didn't result in a failing body, but a body that increased in ability and strength. The older you were, the more able you were."

"That was before the Fall. What about after?" I asked.

"Well, you know about that already. Men had to fall to slumber to be energized for a meager amount of time, about a day. Then he had to sleep again. Valerie is feeling the drain from not sleeping."

"Do people sleep in The Lands of Oblivion much?" I asked.

"All the time." Valerie chimed in. "It is all we can do. We sleep for what feels like years to spend only a few minutes awake before we have to retire to bed again. It is the most we can do."

"That is awful." I said.

Valerie nodded. "I guess I didn't realize until now how pathetic an existence like that is. I thought I had a pretty good deal; I got to rest all the time and didn't have to work!"

Joshua and I chuckled, then Joshua spoke to me. "As soon as her skin touches just a fraction of the light of The Abode, she will be fine for years. Her body will immediately convert the light to energy. It won't just heal her, it will sustain her. This is why you could go into The Lands of Oblivion without feeling any fatigue. You are carrying so much converted light that you would not need to sleep for decades."

"So does anybody sleep in The Abode?" I asked.

"Yes. But not out of necessity. Only if they want to."

"Why would they want to?" I asked.

"There are things to be learned through dreams, and ways to communicate in them that differs from when one is awake." Joshua said as He barreled on down the trail.

Much time passed and nobody spoke. Valerie marched on despite her weariness. After more time passed, we came upon a place in the trail where the light from The Abode was close enough to leak into the blackness of the world we were in. I could see the light in front of us like one can see fog hanging in the air on a cold night. And the moment Valerie walked into it, she quickened her steps. Not long after that I found that the three of us were jogging, Valerie in front, Joshua steering her from behind with the hand he was holding. When she would take a wrong turn He would gently direct her back in the right direction and His voice would chime in from behind her saying, "This is the way." She was literally fleeing from this place.

We eventually made our way out. Valerie was changed even further upon our exit into the fullness of the light, and all that wasn't *her* was burned away. She was transformed into a beautiful woman of stature that took my breath away. I suppose Joshua had the ability to see her like this all along. No wonder He had been so lovestruck by her back in The Lands of Oblivion.

Joshua and I escorted her to The City and Joshua showed her to her mansion, where real gifts from her children lined the walls, tidy and clean. Needless to say, Valerie broke to pieces at the sight of them, joyfully weeping, but that didn't compare to the wonderful meltdown she had when her actual children walked through the door with no bitterness held against her anymore. I watched Joshua smiling while the whole thing unfolded, her children embracing her and telling her how much they loved her. He knew all along that her children were here, but didn't tell her. I walked over to Him as they were all holding each other in the middle of the room.

"Why didn't you tell her they were here?" I asked.

Joshua smiled. "I wanted to surprise her. Plus, she needed to make the decision to leave based on Me rather than them. If she hadn't made the decision based on trust, throwing herself into a risk that demanded full surrender, her resolve wouldn't have held up on the path when she got tired. If she had done it for her kids she would have turned back because while that kind of desire is good, it isn't strong enough to hold up under the weight of darkness in that place. She made it out because she wasn't trusting herself to get through it, but fully trusting Me. She abandoned herself to Me, and that never fails."

We watched for some time, then bowed out quietly, allowing the family to have some alone time.

"You ready for another go?" Joshua said, as we made our way out onto the street outside of the mansion. He lightly patted me on the back as He asked.

"Hell? Yeah." I said without a pause between the words.

Joshua laughed so hard that His head lurched back, pointing His face up towards The Refulgence as His hands planted themselves on His lower back. I loved making Him laugh. He chuckled all the way back to the narrow path.

Fourteen

As we stepped past the foliage that was already growing back and attempting to disguise the entrance to the Lands of Oblivion, I couldn't help but reflect upon everything that had happened in such a short amount of time; my arrival into The Countries of Matrimony, my exploration with Joshua of a few of the higher levels, our decent into darkness, and the redemption of Valerie. It wasn't long ago that I had cut down the bushes I was passing now, and I remembered the suspicion I had about what we were about to do. It turned out that my suspicions were confirmed. We had gone into deep regions and brought someone out. This left a question still unanswered.

"Joshua?" I asked.

"Yes?" He turned to me just as we stepped onto the hidden path.

"I didn't believe that after death a person could be saved."

Initially I thought I was asking a question, but as it escaped my mouth, it came out more as a confession. Mid sentence I realized that it was more of an accusatory statement towards Joshua'a ability to save anyone rather than what I first understood it to be; a doctrinal stance.

"I know. That is one reason why I brought you with Me." He smiled graciously, obviously already aware of my assumption of His inability, but responded patiently, as He always did.

"Why wasn't I taught about this on earth?" I asked.

"Sometimes men do not connect the dots between the most fundamental, foundational truths they believe and the implications of those truths. How can men be saved after they have died? I would say that nothing can separate a person from the love of God. If that isn't true, nothing is. No matter how far a person goes, repentance is always an option."

"I suppose so." I said.

"And by the way," Joshua said out of the corner of His mouth like He was telling me a secret, "Repentance is more about receiving grace than anything else. Repentance flows from the assumption that forgiveness is available."

He winked at me, then continued speaking as I feel in step behind Him, following Him down the blinded path.

"In your past life, if you were to have told theologians that you believed that after death I descend into darkness to rescue them, they would surely demand from you scriptural proof of such a thing. The thought of such a thing would be offensive to them rather than beautiful."

"And what would I have told them? I can't think of any passages that say that You will be rescuing the lost after earth has passed away." I admitted.

"There aren't any. But what theologians forget is that scripture *does* record that I entered hell. And because time works differently here, not following a concrete, consecutive line as it did on earth, if I have been there, then I am there and will be there. This is not a new redemption, but a very old one. As Lewis said, 'All moments have been or shall be were, or are, present in the moment of His descending. There is no spirit in prison to whom He did not preach.'"

"Clive said that?" I said surprisedly.

"Yes. He seemed to be more enlightened to these realities than most." Joshua chuckled. "It is true: Every knee will bow and every tongue confess. And they will do so of their own volition, and out of love."

I thought about what this implied. I suddenly realized that Joshua couldn't be *just* referring to people. Foreign as this was to me, I decided to let Him talk rather than interrupt with another question.

"Again, nothing can separate those I created from My love. What would be the point of conquering death if in return I was not able to reach past it to secure those that I died for?" He paused, as though He really wanted me to answer His question, but I didn't have much of an answer so I stayed quiet, staring back at Him. Then, as though my silence was an answer in and of itself, He said, "I conquered death. This means death has no ability to hinder My plans to save and redeem all in the least bit."

"I had always been taught that hell was a locked door. Inaccessible." I reflected.

"Yeah." Joshua said.

I continued. "And I guess I still think of hell, or whatever you want to call it, in terms of a locked door, but a door that is locked from the inside. People aren't sent there and locked within; those that are there choose it."

"Exactly. Excellently said. This is the door no man can open, at least from the outside. I gave men the keys to heaven long ago, but I possess the keys to hell. Some people think that I have the keys to hell so that I can lock men away there, but there is nothing further from the truth. I have the keys to hell so that I may have entrance to it. Those within try to lock the rest of us out so that we wouldn't be able to, what they call, "pester" them. They want to be left alone, but I refuse to cater to that desire, for it is misled and driven by guilt, shame, and confusion. I will give humans just about anything they desire, but I can't abandon Myself at their request. I am an unrelenting pursuer of those that I love. I cannot stop being who I am. I cannot be untrue to Myself by not pursing each and every creature that I love."

We walked down the rest of the path in silence this time, and the time it took to make it to Ethelwulf's dwelling seemed short compared to our first trip.

We walked past Ethelwulf's and soon Valerie's as well. I could smell both the stale of Ethelwulf's and the mold of Valerie's as we passed.

We walked by many more shanty houses, some more like huts, some not even that. The poverty was astounding and made my stomach churn. It began to occur to me that we were in some kind of town, the buildings randomly dispersed about, with Ethelwulf's house being on the edge of this village of sorts.

Joshua turned us towards one particular house and pointed towards it. A woman was outside, kneeled down and doing something in the dirt alongside the wall to her house.

We walked up behind her, speaking loudly to each other so as not to startle her, but she didn't take any notice to our presence. I walked over and came up beside her so that I could see what she was doing but my curiosity wasn't satisfied by what I saw. She looked like she was playing in the dirt.

"Excuse me." I said.

The woman didn't budge or take any notice.

"*Excuse me.*" I said with more volume and sharpness.

The woman jumped back at the sound of my voice.

"Yes?" She said, shaken.

"What are you doing?" I asked. Joshua was standing back, obviously letting me have a go with this one. He was smiling.

"Fool. What do you think I am doing? Gardening of course!" She snapped.

"Oh, I am sorry. I didn't mean to offend you." I said respectfully. I wanted to treat this woman with the same air of respect and royalty that Joshua demonstrated with Valerie, and I wasn't starting off on the right foot.

"I am *not* offended. You think me to be that weak, eh?" She said as she looked up at me out of the corner of her squinted eyes.

"No! No, I just...." I trailed off, figuring it may be better not to say *anything* rather than something at all.

"Good! I was just between naps and figured that I should plant some of these seeds so that I can get a harvest during summertime. Spring is the time to plant." She said confidently.

I looked around once more, trying to determine how she had come to the conclusion that it was springtime when darkness was the only season that seemed to be at hand.

"I suppose so." I said, trying not to start another argument. I looked at Joshua and shrugged, communicating that I didn't know what else to say. He stepped forward.

"Cecilia." Joshua said.

"Now how the hell do you know my na..." She said as she spun around and stood, facing Joshua. The moment she saw who it was, her voice broke off and she calmed.

"Oh. Its just you." She finished.

"Hello. It is good to see you again." Joshua said.

"Is it? I guess miracles *do* happen." Cecilia said snidely.

"What are you planting?" Joshua asked with real interest in His voice.

"Pole beans. Need something to eat. Nothing to eat around here." She muttered.

"But that is not the only reason why you are growing them, right?" Joshua asked.

"True. Seeing them crawl up the side of the house, blossom, and leaf out until I cannot see their vines anymore..." She trailed off, suddenly staring off into nothingness.

"...Give you life?" Joshua said, bringing her back to consciousness as He finished her sentence for her.

"Yes." She admitted. It was the first moment that I saw her be soft.

"Will they grow?" I asked stupidly, thinking about the lack of sunshine and forgetting how she would inevitably interpret my comment.

"Of course they will grow, fool!" She hissed.

"How?" I asked, motivated to slight defiance by her attitude.

"Light will come!" She yelled at me, staring me down.

Joshua stepped closer to her, drawing her attention from me and onto Him. Again, she calmed.

"We have talked about this before, Cecilia. Did your last bunch of seeds sprout?" Joshua said in a near whisper, so gently and with so much genuine care that one could not help but notice the sensitivity of it.

"No." Cecilia admitted, as her head hung, her chin touching her frail chest. She was a thin woman, medium height, wearing tattered rags like Valerie's.

"Cecilia, what if there was a place where seeds grew into trees in less than a day?" Joshua said with a sparkle of joy in His eyes.

Cecilia looked up quickly, with a look that showed that she was trying to determine if Joshua was pulling an unfair practical joke on her or not. Joshua went on.

"What if there was a place where you could garden in lusciousness? A place where you could plant beans, then in the same day, plant the beans from the harvest? A place where life stumbles over itself, layer upon layer, mile upon mile, stacked up and stretching out into every expanse available? A place where the beauty of creation is like a fountain for you to drink from unceasing?"

"I would find that land and live there forever!" She blurted out, the luring words becoming too much for her to keep back the explosion of her response.

"Follow Me."

"Will you lead me to these lands you speak of?" She questioned as though it was too good to be true.

"Yes." Joshua said confidently.

"I am ready to go. Nothing to pack." She started walking away from the broken house and the small holes she had dug in the dry, rocky ground where she was planning on planting the seeds.

She was about ten feet away when Joshua called out to her, having not taken even one step, "Bethany is there."

Cecilia froze.

"What?" She yelled. Her peace leaked away like a pot filled with water and holes.

"We have gone over this before. Bethany is there in My lands of green." Joshua said.

"Are you kidding? How can you tell me about how great that place is and not tell me the *minor* point that

Bethany is there?" She screamed, with heavy sarcasm in her voice.

"I hoped that since my last visit you would have worked through your feelings towards her. Or that you would at least be more lured by your desires than repelled by your disdain."

"Nothing has changed. Worked through my feelings towards her? Do you remember what she did to me? To my daughter? You have to be joking me! She deserves punishment! And you let her into your lands? What does that say of you about my loss and pain? You lack justice!" She yelled.

"All punishment has been paid for. Justice has been served." Joshua said calmly while His right hand rubbed the palm of His left hand in a way that seemed absentminded or unconscious.

"Ah, that excuse for justice again! I can't stand to hear it. You *know* I cannot allow myself to be in the same room as her! I would vomit." She scoffed as she spit violently at the ground.

"But it is such a large place, much bigger than a room! Surely you can share it!" I blurted out.

"*You* shut up. This is between him and I." She said, and pointed to Joshua.

I was merely attempting to help. I stepped back, deciding I wasn't going to try to persuade her make the right decision anymore. I thought, "*If she wants to be here, fine.*"

"Cecilia, you must forgive her." Joshua pleaded.

"I must not do anything!" She screamed, and with that she ran into her house and came sprinting out with a broom in hand, wildly swinging it around. She came at me, but my body was so full of energy from the light of the Abode that I easily jumped out of the way of the swing aimed for my face. Cecilia then made a direct line for Joshua.

"Time to go!" Joshua yelled out, and we came together, running in the same direction away from her house with Cecilia chasing us.

Cecilia's pain was very real and I wasn't in any way downplaying her agony, but in that bizarre moment, running next to Joshua, the One and Only King, away from a deranged woman with a broom, down in that ridiculous darkness of The Lands of Oblivion, I couldn't help but start laughing hysterically and without restraint. It was all just so absurd; too absurd for any other response. Joshua saw how I was dealing with the moment and began laughing as well. It was as though we were two teenagers that had just toilet papered someone's house in the middle of the night and they had woken up and chased us off. I felt very close to Joshua in that moment. We were thicker than thieves.

After Cecilia had tired, given up chase, and turned around to start walking home, Joshua and I slowed to a walk, then stopped. We were still laughing, but slowly we came around and I began asking Him about Cecilia, because He obviously had interacted with her before.

"So what was all of that about?" I asked while catching my breath, as the air there didn't do much to supply my body with oxygen.

"Cecilia used to be very close to My heart, back in her last life. She would find Me through creation, usually when she was gardening in her backyard. In that setting is where her heart would unfold to not only the created beauty, but the Uncreated beauty. Her eight year old daughter would play with her as she gardened. One day, while Cecilia was lost in beauty, a car pulled up in front of their house. Cecilia wasn't completely paying attention because she was so lost in her own world, enjoying Me. Hours later she came back to herself to find that her daughter, Amelia, wasn't anywhere to be found. Not many days later they found Amelia's body and her killer; Bethany."

"Oh wow."

"Yeah. Every time I go to see Cecilia, she brings up what Bethany did. Bethany and I have already sorted things out, but Cecilia hasn't forgiven Bethany yet, and it has resulted in such a powerful bitterness in Cecilia's heart that she cannot imagine being in The Abode with Bethany."

"I understand that." I said, honestly.

"Yes, I do too. But the greatest tragedy isn't just that Cecilia wants nothing to do with Bethany, but that in not forgiving, she hurts herself. I tell people to forgive others that have wronged them not just because I forgive, but because if people do not forgive, it ruins them from the inside out. Unforgiveness is poison to the heart; it forces one to drink of bitterness and contempt. Cecilia's choice to hold onto her need for Bethany to be punished results in her being cut off from everyone, including her daughter."

"What?"

"Yep. Unforgiveness cuts her off from Me, from those around her, and from her own daughter."

"How so?"

"Well, Amelia has already forgiven Bethany for what she did. Amelia is in the Abode already." Joshua said.

"Why didn't you tell Cecilia that? That seems like a great way to persuade her to come back home." I said, surprised that Joshua hadn't thought of that yet.

"I *have* told her that. Cecilia knows that Amelia is there, waiting for her. But her contempt for Bethany is greater than her love for her own daughter. Her desire for punishment towards the woman that took her daughter is greater than her desire to be reunited with her daughter."

"That is ridiculous." I said.

"Yes it is. That is the nature of unforgiveness. I want her to forgive Bethany so that she can actually be whole and peaceful again. It is high time for her to enjoy her life again and to get out of this place." Joshua said.

"Isn't there anything else we could do?" I asked.

"Yes. There will come a time where I will bring Bethany here to ask for forgiveness. I am hoping that helps. It may just result in another explosion, but it is worth a shot. If that doesn't work, I will ask Amelia to come with Me. That may not work either though, since this isn't about love for Amelia anymore, but anger with Bethany. You know what is ironic?"

"What?"

"Well, when Amelia forgave Bethany, which naturally resulted in her desiring to go with Me to The Abode, we arrived there and Amelia had nobody to mother her. Can you guess who volunteered to step in and play that role until Cecilia comes?"

"You have got to be kidding me." I said.

"Nope. Bethany. And she has done a fantastic job. It has been very healing for both of them. They live in the same mansion. Lets keep that as our little secret though." Joshua winked at me.

"For sure! Can you imagine if Cecilia found out about that? She would flip!" I said, laughing.

"Yes she would!"

Fifteen

"This way. One more visit before we go deeper." Joshua pointed into the blackness again, like He had some unseen compass, showing Him exactly where to go.

"Deeper?" I asked.

"Yes. There are others, far more lost than those here in The Lands of Oblivion." He said.

More lost? I thought to myself, wondering how people could be more lost than Cecilia and Ethelwulf. Our record so far wasn't outstanding either, one out of three, and if people were more lost where we were headed next, I wondered how effective we would be.

"If they are more lost than those here, won't it just be harder to bring them back to The Abode than it was with Cecilia or Ethelwulf? How will we succeed in bringing *any* back?" I asked.

"Our motive is love. Our goal is not primarily to bring them back. I don't want anyone to come before they are ready. I am in no rush. I *will* win each. Remember, we have all of eternity to do this. Their ability to rebel is not greater than My ability to love them. I win every time." Joshua replied.

"Wait a second. Our motive isn't to bring them back?" I said, caught a bit off guard.

"No. It never has been. The Bride's commissioning was always first and foremost to love. When that is the motive, the rest falls into place perfectly. But when there is an agenda other than love it becomes something it shouldn't be. I feel no urgency or pressure to get people out. Don't mistake Me; I want them out. I want them with Me. I want them not in pain and despair. More than you could ever imagine. But I also know how this story ends, and the unwavering persistence of My love. They *will* eventually be led out. It is up to them if that happens sooner or later. When a person's motive isn't trying to get more notches on their belt or fear that someone's salvation is solely their responsibility, then they are able to really love people. Until then they will only be a salesman, not a minister. After all, a person can't sell something that is free.

Remember, I am not driven by a need to change people, but to love people. My love will make any changes that need to be made. It will happen naturally."

"Ok." I said as I took in what He was saying. I had always been an evangelist of sorts, using whatever methods I could to get the person to say a prearranged prayer of repentance and confession. Now that I looked back on that, it seemed superficial and plastic. I suddenly realized that there wasn't a point at which I could remember the original disciples praying any such prayer, thus I could not determine the exact point at which they were "saved". This was slightly disconcerting, but also comforting. Maybe their salvation came through knowing Joshua rather than a precise moment where they prayed a three sentence prayer. Maybe.

"Wouldn't it just be easier to just force them out of hell? Just pick them up and carry them out?" I asked.

Joshua smiled. "Probably. But did you see the swing Cecilia had with that broom? It could shake a molar loose!" We both laughed.

"But seriously," Joshua continued, still smiling. "They would just run back to the darkness. They have to decide for themselves not to be here anymore or it doesn't hold up. It is much like someone checking themselves into a rehabilitation clinic. They have to decide for themselves that they want to get help. Nobody can decide for them. But in this case, instead of checking in to get help, they check out."

"But because You are sovereign, aren't You really just allowing them to stay here by not forcefully executing Your will? I said.

"I am not *allowing* them to stay here, just as I did not *allow* sin in the beginning. *Allowance* must be understood within the context of the power men have in being able to make their own choices. Once it is, one realizes that I value men's freedom over having a picture perfect family. The same goes for what men refer to as sovereignty; It must be grasped in the context of choice, lest it turn into a complete misunderstanding of My character."

"Like?"

Oh, take your pick! That I sit back and allow evil. That was one doctrine that men paraded. Another was even more unbelievable; that I even orchestrate and ordain evil."

"What?"

"Well, some people's view of sovereignty led them to believe that I am behind every event that occurred on earth. I probably don't have to remind you that while that included a load of wonderful things, it also included events like the reign of Pol Pot, the gas chambers in Auschwitz, and every abortion ever executed. And you can see how they came to those conclusion when one doesn't understand the difference between having all authority and having all *control.*

True sovereignty looks very different from what some men assumed. My desires *are* going to come to pass, even in light of men's ability to choose, that part they got right. What it is not is a winning out through a domineering or controlling sort. And especially not through other, even less fitting, avenues that men have regarded Me capable of like destruction and murder.

No, this whole thing will be made right because each will *choose* it, not because of intimidation, but because I will win each and every one of them over through unmerited kindness.

And I said I value freedom over a perfect family, but I must add, we will get there. We *will* be a perfect family!" Joshua said jovially.

We continued walking into the darkness, hanging like a veil in front of us and impossible to see through fully. The closer we came to the house the more we could make it out, the way it is for a person when they are navigating through thick fog in the middle of the night.

"This one just arrived. I haven't gotten a chance to greet him yet." Joshua said.

Joshua walked up to the door and knocked. On the door was a small door knocker with a plaque on it that read, "You were a stranger and you welcomed me in." Joshua didn't use the knocker.

The door cracked open slightly as a result of the knock.

"Can I help you?" A shadowed face asked us through the two inch crack.

"Hello!" Joshua said cheerfully.

"Um, hi." The man's voice dropped in tone, as though he was disappointed.

We stood there for a few awkward moments of silence, the hospitable invitation not coming forth like we had expected, then Joshua asked meekly, "Could we come in?"

"I am not sure I am completely comfortable with that. I have had people come to my door before, and it usually pertained to religious matters." He said through the opening in the door, making the only movement I could see being his lips moving slowly on the other side of the door.

"Oh! I assure you we are not here for religious reasons." Joshua said.

The man snorted and said, "We'll see. They always come with reading materials and such, not knowing that I studied in seminary and can debate the best of them into a corner. I suppose you can come in."

The door swung open and the man walked over to a chair in the corner of the room and sat down. He was better dressed than the others, with no rips or holes in his shirt or pants. I realized that this was probably because he hadn't arrived long ago, and his clothes hadn't had the time to wear out yet.

All along the walls were shelves tacked up and overflowing with books. The house looked more a library than it did a place to live.

"So. If you aren't here for religious reasons, why are you here?"

"I wanted to introduce Myself." Joshua said, walking over to the man in the chair and extending His hand.

"My name is Joshua. Very nice to meet you, my friend." Joshua said.

The man shook Joshua's hand and said, "Nice to meet you too. My name is Mark."

"Just arrive?" Joshua said.

"Yes, not sure how long ago, but not long. Still getting settled in. Do you know what this place is?" Mark asked.

"Yes. This place is referred to as The Lands of Oblivion." I said.

The man's eyebrows elevated for a moment, then plummeted back to sea level, briefly showing something that looked like disbelief.

"Is there a problem?" Joshua asked.

"No, not exactly. I guess I didn't expect where I would end up to have such a drab name, though it *is* fitting for this place, isn't it? I imagined that I would end up somewhere brighter. More glorious." Mark said, looking puzzled.

"Well there are brighter places, definitely." Joshua said.

"Yeah? How do I get there?" Mark asked.

"I am the Way. Follow Me." Joshua said.

"Sir, I just met you. I am still settling in. My books need to be ordered and alphabetized. I didn't realize that going to a brighter place would involve following an utter stranger to get there." Mark said with an air of snideness.

"That is the problem." I said.

"What do you mean 'that is the problem'?" Mark said, looking offended.

"Well, after reading all of these books on various doctrines, theologies, and interpretation techniques, this is the first time you have met Joshua. You don't recognize who He is. *That* is the problem." I said frankly.

"I am confused. Should I have met you before this moment?" Mark said, eyebrows summiting Everest again.

"Yes. He has always been available. Your study and books have not led you closer to The Eternal, but further away." I said directly, wondering how Mark would handle such straightforward communication.

"Ha! My mother tried to tell me the same thing. Believe what you want. I am only concerned with truth." Mark said, waving away the point.

"Tell me this, Mark. When you died, what happened?" Joshua asked.

"That *was* peculiar. Funny you bring that up. A being stood in front of me, encased in light, and said one simple thing to me; "I love you." This was very odd to me, as I was aware of the righteous life that I had lived, thus didn't know why this being would need to communicate this to me, as I already knew it. I had already earned love for the things that I had done. That issue was settled. That alone made me question who was talking to me. After all, I couldn't clearly see their face."

As Mark looked off into the distance, obviously pondering that moment, Joshua and I looked at each other, both making a "Oh no" face.

Mark snapped back to consciousness and continued. "I thought to myself, '*Where is the judgement?*' That was a big red flag as well. All I could sense was goodness and love. Only goodness? Only love? Where was the wrath? Where was the fear? Where was the hard to stomach *truth?* Don't give me some watered-down god! I want the real thing! I know that first and foremost god hates who you are, *then* comes the determining if a due propitiation is in place to cover the transgressions and thus steer the hatred in another direction. Love? Ha! I knew this pansy god was nothing of what I know the one true God to be. See, I am a teacher and pastor. I have a whole network of churches that adhere to whatever I teach. I have to get it right because judgement is stricter for me, you see? I knew that this feminized, sissy, spineless, hippy god wasn't God at all! I was wiser than that. I quickly deduced that this was in fact an angel of light, as scripture warns us about. I thought to myself,

'*This is not God! This is a devil!*' I had to look past what I thought I was seeing and see reality. I had to discern darkness when it shrouded itself in light. It was the ultimate test."

Mark sat back in his chair, wearing a face nothing short of gloating. I swallowed, not from anxiety, but just in anticipation of the inevitable bomb that was about to be dropped. The wake-up call this guy was about to receive was going to be a doozy, even though being in The Lands of Oblivion should have been sufficient enough to clue him into the fact that he may have gotten things a bit off.

"That *was* the judgement." Joshua said gently.

"Excuse me? I am not sure if I heard you correctly." Mark said, cupping his hand to his ear, the gloating face quickly turning into appall mixed with surprise.

"After everything was taken into consideration, *that* was the judgement. That I love you."

"That *you* love me? I am confused. You?" Mark said.

"Yes. It was I that stood before you that day." Joshua said calmly.

I thought about everything Mark had just said, not knowing he had been saying them about Joshua. Pride results in a person's foot being stuck in their mouth more often than not. And for most men, what Mark had said would have been fighting words, but Joshua didn't even seem to notice. True humility results in confidence that is impossible to offend.

"Was it? How would I ever be sure of that? Show me some empirical evidence!" Mark was shouting now, obviously riled up from the embarrassment of insulting Joshua so blatantly.

"Truth is not a doctrine or philosophy. It is a Person." I said, pointing to Joshua. "You want fear? How about this? What if you have it all backwards? What if all of your wisdom is foolishness in actuality? What if The Eternal is only good, with no wrath or punishment in Him? What if you missed it completely? What if His justice is more about restoration than it is punishment?" I felt heat rush to my face. I wasn't angry, but this discourse definitely got my blood pumping.

Mark sat there quiet.

"My grace and love are not weaknesses, or, how did you say it? Sissy? Pansy?" Joshua said seriously, for it was a very serious moment, then His face started to break, like He was trying to hold an emotion back but wasn't doing very well at resisting it. Then, like a crack in a dam gives way to a surge, He surrendered to laughter. The thought that Joshua was weak was amusing, and I began laughing too. Mark didn't laugh.

"My love and grace are the strongest forces in existence." Joshua continued, still recovering from being called a sissy for having the power to value those without value. "Your 'truth' is what is weak, because it lacks grace. It is powerless. Doctrines formulated out of self-righteousness and unbelief never liberated anyone from sin, thus they lack power. *You* lack power. You want the most courageous, masculine, rugged, strong, undefeatable, characteristic in all of existence? You want power? Get love." Joshua said.

Mark continued in his silence. I have to admit, I liked that.

Then something that I wasn't expecting happened. Light started to radiate from Joshua more than usual. It started slow, but was obviously gaining speed. Immediately I felt the beginning of the joyful discomfort that came from the light when I was in the upper regions of The Countries of Matrimony. The volume of radiance that Joshua usually allowed to escape from Him had dramatically increased, and now rays of light reached out from Him like liquid flames, whipping around like fire does when challenged by the wind. His garments were not made of materials like silk or cotton, but woven strands of pure light, resembling gold. His eyes were bright white, beaming, looking directly at Mark. Everything in that little house suddenly felt immaterial, as though the light was a more solid and real substance than anything around us. The dirt, the walls, the books, Mark's body, everything; it all seemed to suddenly be swallowed up in light. All there was to notice was Joshua. All one could acknowledge was Him.

"I love you." Joshua said. His voice pulsed out from Him with force, sounding like the crashing of waves on the north shore of an island positioned in the middle of the ocean's currents. His voice possessed the power that could crush the strongest man, but it drifted into my heart as gently and as refreshingly as a slow moving creek on a hot day.

Like an earthquake had taken ahold of him and thrown him to the floor, Mark crumpled as Joshua's words slammed into him. He shakily got on his hands and knees and slowly, reverently, crawled to Joshua's feet. He was weeping.

"Thank you!" Mark choked out.

Joshua reached down, the brightness dissipating and becoming more of a soft glow now, and hooked His hands under Mark's arms. Without Mark's consent, Joshua forcefully lifted Mark to his feet, the two of them suddenly eye to eye.

"Now you know it was I that stood before you. Now you know that I love you not because of what you have done, but because I love you. I love you because I love you because I love you. Now you know that my judgement is more based upon what I did than what you did.

And I can keep up the shining as long as you like. I *can* reveal Myself. But I do not want you to just be able to recognize that I am *the* one and only Deity only when I am unmasked and revealed. I want people to be able to recognize Me in the simple, in the smallness, in the cup of cold water, in the beggar, in the child. Find Me in others so that you can value someone other than yourself. No more finding Me *only* in the sovereign moments or sovereign doctrines. I am not so limited as to only be able to show up in fireworks and splendor. I am the Lowly Splendor; He who can come in the earthquake or in the whisper, but more often than not, in the whisper. Men seem to forget that it is more of a miracle for something Big to be unveiled through something small than it is for something Big to be seen as it is: big.

Mark, I want to talk with you face to face as one would with a friend. There will be times in the future, when you have grown more, when you will be more ready for the radiance. When you are ready, it won't hinder your ability to interact with Me face to face. Until then, your instinct will be to fall at My feet over and over. And while I understand that, My desire is to reign *with* you. I want to talk *with* you, not just to you."

Mark quickly nodded in agreement.

"Now, it is time for you to leave. It is time for you to stop with your idolatry and come with us."

"Idolatry? Sir, what idolatry are you referring to?" Mark asked respectfully.

"Your books, your studying. Study has been your god. You have thought that you have been studying Me, but you were just studying what other's said about Me. To study Me you have to be in the same room with Me. Knowledge was your god rather than letting the knowledge *of* God lead you closer *to* God. It is time for you to finally set all of your studying aside and come into a relationship with Me." Joshua said with finality.

"Can I take any of my books with me?" Mark said.

"None. It is obviously your choice, but you can only receive all of what you heart desires when all of your diversions are abandoned. A container can only be filled up as much as it is first emptied. And you are one that is not satisfied with 99 percent. You want it all. Don't you?" Joshua replied.

"Yes. But what about this one?" Mark pulled a thick book off one of the nearby shelves on the wall. It looked to be the Book of ancient writs that I had memorized so fervently when I was with the Chosen.

"No. Especially not that book. Like anything else, when that book ceases to lead people into encountering Me it can become more harmful than good, even an idol. There are times when a person may be called to lay aside the word so that he can more fully embrace the Word. That season is upon you."

Mark looked surprised, even confused.

"You do not need to study that book right now. Simply study Me. Gaze upon Me. You have no need for it. It is the word of God, but you now you possess the Word Himself. I am a greater, more supreme authority than those pages could ever contain. Why settle for less? Why settle for the menu when you can eat the food that the menu talks about?"

Mark stared down at the book he held in his hands, then looked at Joshua, then back down at the book. He was clearly thinking it through. Finally, He slowly walked back over to the book shelf and slid the book back into its spot.

Joshua smiled. "Are you ready?"

"Yes. Lets go." Mark said decidedly.

We walked out of Mark's house and towards Ethelwulf's. Mark was about five paces behind Joshua and I, following us.

"He thought you were the devil!" I whispered into Joshua's ear, giggling. "How on earth did he ever come to that conclusion?"

"Crazy isn't it? Some men look for heresy more venomously than truth. And that which you give attention to is what you will perceive. Attention is a form of worship. Whatever you are impressed by, whatever you continually give your attention to, you worship. If you are continually focused on what the enemy has done rather than what The Eternal has done and is doing, you will begin to see the enemy's work in situations where he is not present. Revivalists of old learned how to see God in the darkest of situations and places, and thus found Him there. Power is not necessarily found in discerning darkness, but discerning light. Even policemen know this to be true. Back on earth, they did not study counterfeit bills in order to recognize a fake, but instead would spend their time looking over a real hundred dollar bill. Once you know what the real thing looks like, you can easily dismiss the fakes. Mark never studied the real thing, so when the real thing came along he mistook it for a fake. That is what religion does to people. They mistaken The Eternal for the devil and the devil for The Eternal."

"How can You assure that people will see You as You are?" I asked.

"I can't. They will see Me however their heart allows them to. Mark even recognized love and goodness flowing from Me, but that didn't help his discernment but ironically played against it." Joshua frowned at the thought. Then He smiled as He said, "Maybe I should appear to the theologians as the devil when they come before Me. Maybe *then* they would would call me God!"

We both laughed. I looked back at Mark, hoping he didn't hear what we were saying. Mark's focus was elsewhere. He looked very tired.

"Mark? Are you ok?" I asked.

"I am very tired. This walking is taking it out of me." He said.

"I thought you were a fighter! Pony up, man!" I said, slapping him on the back the way tough guys do.

Joshua didn't seem to take notice to what I said. Instead, He came up beside Mark and lifted his left arm over His head and across his shoulders.

"You want to get the other side?" Joshua asked me.

"I think he has got this." I said.

"Please." Joshua said.

I found myself hesitating for a moment, then hoisted Mark's right arm over my head and grabbed his hand, lifting up on his body, taking his weight upon myself and minimizing the effort he had to put towards walking. It was an awkward way to walk, and Joshua was clearly strong enough to easily carry Mark, but He didn't do so. I wondered if it was because Joshua knew that Mark probably wouldn't appreciate being carried like that. Most wounded soldiers would rather limp off the war field than be carried out.

"You are almost there." Joshua said a few minutes later. "You can do it."

Then it struck me, what was unconscious suddenly becoming conscious; I didn't want Mark to be in The Abode. I had gone into the depths to bring him out but when I was honest about it, I didn't really *like* him. Valerie was easier to like because she simply did not act like she had it together. She was an obvious, literal, mess.

Ethelwulf was deceived in a way that made him just plain pathetic. One couldn't help but feel as though they were interacting with a hurting child when talking to him. Cecilia had lost her daughter in an unbelievable, horrible way. It was easy to feel compassion for them. It was easy to understand why they were the way they were and to cut them slack. But Mark was different. He hadn't been dealt a bad hand in life. He didn't have an excuse for being pompous and self-righteous.

As I lugged Mark's heavy body along, his wheezing breaths just inches from my ear, bringing him closer and closer to the light that would give him the ability to carry his own weight, I heard in my head, or maybe it was in my heart, "He is just as religious as I was."

In less than an instant my memory came forth and reminded me all of the self-righteousness and pride I had walked in before I met Joshua. I remembered how I thought I was happy and content until I was violently pulled out of religion and into grace and got an objective viewpoint on myself and realized that I had no real joy or freedom at all. This must be how Mark felt, whether he knew it or not. He was desperate for the real. He was starved for authentic love. He was thirsty for grace. He was like everyone else.

Joshua had been patient with me in all of my religion. Without it, I would still be lost. It was time for me to do the same for someone else. It would be a double standard to condemn Mark for the way he was, as I had been the same. Just moments after hearing those words echo through my head, all I could feel for him was compassion. Maybe even love.

"Yeah, you can do it Mark. We've got you." I said encouragingly.

"Thank you. I could never do this on my own." Mark said.

I was surprised to see tears dripping down his face. At that moment I realized that Mark must have been much more in touch with his inability than I had first thought. Something significant had happened when Joshua had transfigured back at his house. Encounter does that.

As Mark's tears sunk into my mind, I resined myself to not judge or assume where someone's heart was at, no matter how religious they were. Mark had just proved to me that I was, more often than not, mistaken in my "discernment". Maybe he and I weren't that different after all.

Sixteen

We had ushered Mark back to the light, where he went sprinting into the Abode, full of life and joy, laughing like a little boy as he vanished from sight over a small hill that sat between us and The City. I decided that I did like him after all.

Joshua and I walked back down the path, talking about this and that, and made our way back through the village of shadows where Cecilia and Ethelwulf still stayed. We continued walking until the buildings ceased to spring up before us out of the darkness, making our way into territory that was new, at least to me.

We now came up to what looked like a wall that stood as high and wide as my eyes could see in the failing shadowlight. It was blacker than the blackness around us, clearly flat like you would expect a wall to be, but when I reached out to feel the surface of it, it turned out to not be a wall at all, at least not solid in the way most walls are. My hand sunk through the flat surface as a chilling cold crept up my arm, and I yanked my hand back from it immediately. If darkness could become material, this is what the wall was composed of. It was obviously meant to keep people on one side of it, both by visual and physical means.

Joshua didn't say anything in response to my jerking back my arm, like He wasn't surprised at my reaction. Instead He simply looked at me, then moved towards the wall. He got closer and closer, keeping His pace, and walked headstrong into the wall. One moment He was there, and the next, vanished. The wall had swallowed Him like a fish does a unsuspecting bug resting on the surface of a lake in the ebony of night.

I did not handle this well at all. Immediately I started to panic, it being the first time I couldn't see Joshua near me.

"Just do as I did." Joshua voice came quietly from the other side of the wall, slightly muted and muffled by the semi-material wall.

I walked forward, involuntarily closing my eyes and holding my breath as I felt the cold, even wetness maybe, slide over me and fall off behind me. I was on the other side. Joshua was standing there smiling, waiting for me.

The light was different on the other side of the wall. It was more bright than The Lands of Oblivion had been, but that wasn't much to account for. There was still a lingering feeling of inescapable shadow, but now, for reasons I was not yet aware of, everything had a reddish-orange tint upon it. This was the half-light that made this place less dark than The Lands of Oblivion, but it was a light that did not make you feel like things were any more illuminated just because you could *see* more. It was an eerie light, a dying light. It caused you to squint even more than one does in utter darkness because your mind was sure that if you just focused your eyes enough, you would be able to map out your surroundings. After a minute or two I realized that was not the case; a dead-end effort.

Stretched out before us was one of the more peculiar sights that I had seen yet. The only thing that was being illuminated by the expired light was a staircase, as straight and wide as the wall behind us, which still stretched out as a wall behind us as far as I could see to either side. I had a distinct feeling that the wall had no end. The stairs stretched out before us and did not lead upwards, but down. They plotted such a violent plunge into the nothingness below that it caused me a moment of dizziness just by looking at it. They looked endless. It was as though they went down forever, and if this place had a bottom, I assumed this staircase would eventually collide with it.

"We are going down there?" I asked, as there was nowhere else to go.

"Yes we are. This is The Abyss. Quite a walk. You ready?" Joshua said.

"No." I chuckled, part serious, part sarcastically. "By the way...How do we expect to be any more successful in this place when we only got two out of four back there?" I asked as I pointed back to the wall.

"Two out of four isn't bad." Joshua said encouragingly. "Remember, this is years and years of bondage and twisted thinking that we are dealing with. Their issues don't always come unraveled immediately or easily. Even so, we got two. With Mark, forty-five years of deception were dismantled in the matter of twenty minutes. Love is, most assuredly, more powerful than lies. Thus, while the inhabitants of these regions are wrapped in years of falsity, one moment of encounter can change all of that. Take Paul for example. And for those that don't recognize an encounter when I show up, I continue to intercede on their behalf. I continue to visit, love, and persuade men out of their delusions and out of these lost regions."

Joshua took the first step downward, and I followed suite. Immediately I felt something grab my lungs, as though the little air that I was getting from my surroundings now was cut in half and I was now slightly struggling to get the oxygen I needed. That is, until the next step was taken, when the available air was apparently cut in half again. With the first step I had wondered if I was imagining something, but now it was no longer a fallacy that my mind was making up; I was clearly losing more and more oxygen step by step. It was much like the way a person feels when starting to climb higher elevations, say past 15,000 feet on earth. When someone is that far above the earth, air is thin and a few steps upward can exhaust a person easily, causing the legs to burn with the thirsting of muscles for oxygen.

But we continued. With every step I was acutely aware of my reserves being halved, soon with just a fraction of what I started with at the top of the stairs, which was already only a fraction of what I had felt when in The Abode. Yet, despite this drought in my chest, somehow I was able to keep on. Joshua seemed unaffected.

"Do...you...feel...that?" I choked out. I didn't see how I could keep up the walking for even talking was nearly unbearable, even though I had been filled with light not long ago and could still feel my body full of energy.

"Ah! Yes, I forgot about that. I felt the same thing the first time I came, but I am used to it now. Your body will adjust. This place cannot truly affect you; It cannot harm you. This place, as well as its inhabitants, like to try to pull the wool over people's eyes and tell them they are sick when they are not, or that they can't breath when they can. I have seen many keel over from "heart attacks", when they were just the symptoms of a heart attack, not the real thing at all. As for the air, the facade will fall away. Ignore it and give it no gratification through your struggle or attention."

As Joshua spoke, I felt my lungs relax, maybe because of some physical affect of His words on my body, maybe because I consciously forced my body to loosen up *because* of His words. Either way, He was the instigator of my peace. I started taking deep breaths despite the emptiness that they pulled in, and decided that even if Joshua was wrong and I fell over and passed out, He would know what to do to bring me around again. Soon, within a short amount of time, I wasn't thinking about the air at all anymore, it just as draining and insufficient as ever, but somehow I was now transcending its influence.

Down went the stairs, plummeting further and further away from the Lands of Oblivion, the path, and Abode. We put more and more distance between us and the light. It began to feel more like we were sinking deep into a bottomless sea, even drowning, drifting away from air and light and life. There was no hope here. Everything beautiful was nonexistent. That is, except for Joshua of course. He walked on, maybe almost skipping down the steps like a boy heading downstairs on Christmas morning. Hope is an understatement. He didn't merely hope, He *knew*.

After what seemed to be years of walking, the stairs stopped plunging down and became flat. On either side of the cement-looking route rose walls that were about seven feet in height. Along the walls were black, steel doors, each with a small grated window at eye level. The corridor with doors went for quite a ways straight out from us, then in the distance looked to stop suddenly. Right past the point where I could no longer see any more doors or cement path, the light looked brighter. It was clear that the source of the orangish hue that had lit up the staircase on our way down and now gave enough light to see the corridor of doors was coming from that area, but it was not something I wanted to look at. It was not a light that I was drawn to, but a light that caused my heart to grieve and my eyes to look away. That light made me feel as though every evil thing ever conceived was born in that flickering, dying light. I instinctively knew that all that existed over in that twilight was gratuitous violence, extreme perversion, and bitterness that would cause the most sweet thing to crumble into decay. Death itself originated in that lambency.

I shuttered and turned to Joshua, looking away from the end of the path.

"I do *not* want to go over there."

"You don't need to. We can tackle that later." Joshua said.

"Later? I'm not so sure about that." I said, glancing back at the wobbling dimness.

Joshua chuckled. "It isn't as bad as it likes to present itself. Fear and intimidation is all one is left with when they no longer possess real authority."

"I still don't think I am ready for that. Just looking over there makes my skin crawl."

"I know. Don't concern yourself with that right now. We have other priorities right now. The Eternal knows the exact when and where. We just do as He does."

"And where is He leading now?" I asked.

"You tell me." Joshua said.

I looked around, taking in my surroundings a bit more thoroughly now. There were so many metal doors, all only a few feet apart.

"How about this one?" I pointed to a door nearby.

"Number 43. Very good. Lets take a crack at it."

Joshua went over to the door and looked through the grated window. The opening was only about three inches high, and six inches wide, leaving just enough space to see through the gap with both eyes. Joshua looked through it for a bit, then got on His tip-toes and called inside.

"You there? Can we come in?"

We both fell silent, waiting for a response, but nothing came. Just as Joshua was rising up on His toes again, an echoing hiss shot out through the window, like thousands of voices had just said the same inaudible word at the same time.

"What was that?" I asked.

"That was his response. Not exactly a merry welcome, I suppose." Joshua said. He looked eager, even exhilarated by the eerie sound, wearing a face that was similar to the way a man looks when someone calls out to him across a parking look in an attempt to lure him into a fight.

"Lets go in there." Joshua said, a twinkle of holy rebellion dancing in His eyes.

"You first!" I said.

"You got it." He said.

And with that, Joshua reached out and stuck His fingers through the small window, firmly gripping what He could of the door. I imagine He would have grabbed a doorknob or door handle if there had been one, but the door lacked both. The metal door was completely flat, giving a person nothing to hold on to if they were wanting to get inside.

With a few fingers from each hand inside the window, Joshua began to pull on the door in an attempt to open it. Like tin foil, the three-inch thick door began to bend as though it had been heated to red hotness, and Joshua began to pull it apart as easily as a child tears paper. It was effortless.

I knew Joshua was strong, but in that moment I realized that I had very little understanding of His strength. As I watched the door come apart before Him I experienced a kind of high that I had never experienced before. My heart beat the wall of my chest like it wanted out. It was a sort of terror that gripped me; an awe that came from witnessing such a strength. I was not concerned per say, as though He would ever turn that kind of power towards me, but a sobriety came over me of what He was capable of. Beholding such power was elating, and I knew that this was only a portion of what He could do. Nothing could stand before Him and hinder His ability to love those He was after. He cannot be hidden from. He cannot be escaped from. He hunts down all and is merciless in His pursuit. He will stop at nothing.

I knew His gentleness, but I had not seen how brutal He could be to something that was standing in the way of His love. The door was now fragments strewn about on the ground around us. Dust flew about in the air, and a large hole in the side of the wall now lurked before us, black inside.

Joshua stepped through the hole, the cloud of dust from the broken rubble still hanging in the air, and I stepped in behind Him.

Seventeen

The screaming was deafening. I couldn't think, see, or walk. I reached out my hand, felt Joshua's back, and steadied myself by gripping His garments. I could hear Him speaking something very quietly that was somehow louder than the thousands of voices that I could hear agonizingly screeching in horror. It was the worst sound I had ever heard. Like an orchestra crescendos and dives together in unison, the voices were grouped together and following the same pattern, only more like verbal bleeding than strings and horns making music. The sound spun around me like the wind, weaving around my body and hemming me in from all sides. I hated it.

And suddenly the sound, or more accurately, the sounds, stopped. Joshua had just finished His sentence, and when He did, all fell quiet.

I opened my eyes, a little dizzy from the auditory ambush, and looked around cautiously to see the masses that had just produced such a blood curtailing noise. I was surprised to see that the room, or cell, was so small, implicating that it was impossible for thousands of people to be housed in this much space. All I saw was one man in a corner a few feet away, hidden in the shadows and balled up in the fetal position. I concluded that such a sound could never be produced by any *man,* and that most likely, I wasn't standing in the presence of a mere *human*.

"Now that is better. Hello my friend. I believe we have met before." Joshua said kindly.

"Yes. We have. Speak quickly. I know not how long they will stay quiet." The being said in a hiss, spittle flying through the air as it spoke.

"They will stay quiet as long as I want to talk." Joshua said confidently.

"What do you want?" It said, looking up. I saw its eyes, glowing eyes, like the eyes of a nocturnal animal when the headlights of a car shine on them in the darkness of night. Whatever it was, it was not beautiful.

"I have come for you." Joshua said.

"You want me?" It croaked.

"Why wouldn't I? We still desire your input and service. There is still much work to be done. You still have a destiny. But only with Me. It has been far too long. You have forgotten what it is like in The Countries of Matrimony."

"True."

"And you have always pondered why I listened to you and granted your request instead of sending you away. That cost those farmers all of their wealth. That many pigs is not a small matter. Some have wondered why I would do that for your kind."

"The farmers got over it." It said, waving the comment away.

"True."

"But yes. You have a point. You were..." its voice gurgled, like it was choking to annunciate the word, "*gracious*. Even to me and those I lord over. Because of that, I always wondered if You...." it looked away in hopeful shame as it paused, as though what it was about to say was too good to be true, "...cared about me."

Joshua was quiet.

Maybe Joshua's silence was interpreted by the creature as confirmation that Joshua didn't care, dashing its brittle hopes, but whatever it interpreted from the silence, it was too much. Its suddenly snapped its head back, looking directly at us and it bitterly spat out, "But I, we, ended up here anyways, didn't I?"

Joshua retort was instant. "Pity will not help you, and it does not motivate Me. I am already motivated; you do not need pity. Ending up here was your decision. Nobody told you to set up camp here."

Now it was the thing's turn to be silent, the charge obviously true.

"You asked if I wanted you. I do. Do you want to come with Me?" Joshua said.

"I am not so opposed. You are the only one that I have ever encountered that has given me, us, grace. Even in our kingdom, amidst what we call allies, there is hatred and betrayal. Never grace. And even our kind need of that substance You call grace. It is what sustains a thing. Without it we must feed off anything created in Your image." It twitched, shaking its head back and forth so fast that it seemed it may cause the head to detach from the neck. This disgusting thing gave me the same feeling that the light at the end of the corridor did.

"But what of them?" It said, pointing to its chest.

"Let them decide for themselves." Joshua said.

The being stood up and took a step out of the shadows and into the light. If black was not a color but a material, that is what it was. Its skin was broken and haggard, covered in boils and deep gashes, like someone had whipped it everyday for a thousand years Nothing about it was symmetrical, as though the parts of its body came from different places rather than born together in a group. One leg was clearly shorter than the other. One arm was long and skinny and the other was short and muscled. Its eyes were not placed at the same height. Sometimes it lacked something altogether, like its left ear in this case. The description "unattractive" was not sufficient to communicate the extensiveness of the destination that I felt when I looked upon it. And that was just the little I could see in the dim light. The smell, which had assaulted my nose when we came through the hole, reminded me of what I imagined the result of giardia and bile combined would smell like. It was so bitter in the air that it burned the insides of my nostrils when I inhaled. I tried to breathe through my mouth to help with the smell, but I started to taste the smell then, and resorted back to breathing through my nose. I was so repulsed in both sight and smell that a little throw up filled my throat involuntarily, and I quickly swallowed it back down and hoped that the thing didn't notice. Oddly enough, what filled my mouth was more accommodating to my senses than the smell that hung in the air around us.

"I want to be beautiful again. " It said.

Joshua stepped forward.

"Joshua, wait!" I exclaimed. Without thinking about it, I grabbed His hand and pulled Him outside the cell into the hallway.

"You can't be serious! You are going to let that *thing* come with us?" I said.

"That *thing* used to command whole legions of angels."

"Yeah! It looks like it still is!" I exclaimed.

"Scythe, if this is shocking to you, then you are in for much bigger surprises soon." Joshua said, laughing.

I wasn't really in the mood for laughter, and the moment was not one that called for joy, but when Joshua started laughing I realized how ridiculous it was to ever be anything *but* joyful. Seriousness didn't survive well around Joshua, at least not the kind of seriousness I was distributing. Love can be serious, like Joshua had been with Valerie, but joy is never far below the surface of real love. Love without joy is not love.

Who Joshua is was taking shape inside my head and heart more and more. He wasn't just Lord, Savior, and Bridegroom. He was the guy that interrupts a "reverent" service by playing with kids in the back. He was the guy that would fall out of His seat during mass, laughing hysterically when nobody had told a joke. He was the carrier of joy. He *was* joy.

Joshua continued. "The beauty and power he was given can only be matched by a few. It is time for his place to be restored. We have been waiting for him since he chose to leave and plummet to the Great Depths. He was created for a purpose up above, and that need and purpose can only be fulfilled by him. To not include him would result in a loss for the rest of us. He has much to contribute. Not even for a second will I entertain the idea of not including someone that I created, human or not."

I had learned from Joshua's ability to see Valerie as she not yet was that He had a knack at seeing someone's true identity and worth when nobody else did, even the person themselves. It was wrong of me to second guess Him.

"I know *You* know what you are doing. I just don't always know what You are doing. I am not always very quick on the uptake. I'm sorry I drug you out here." I said.

"I am doing the same thing with him that I did with you. Who is to determine how far is too far gone?" Joshua asked.

"I know. I am sorry. Go ahead."

"Why thank you!" Joshua said, smiling like I had just given *Him* permission to do what He wanted to do. We both knew He could do whatever He wanted and it made the moment slightly humorous, taking the intensity out that I had just instilled into the situation. I followed Him back into the tiny, cement cell and faced the being that stood in the back of the dank hole.

"We are ready. Let us go." Joshua said.

"Wait." It said, as it dropped to its knees. "Joshua, You are Lord."

I did not expect this sudden admission, but what followed, I expected even less. I was not aware that such a simple, calm confession could result in so much immediate turmoil. The moment those blessed words escaped its mouth, nothing short of an explosion decimated from its body. The best way to describe it is to say that it was similar to the way that obsidian shatters into pieces of sharp black glass fragments when struck with a large sledgehammer. Things, undefinable things that were jet black, went flying out from him in all directions, filling the room. There was no screaming as before, but their flight was deafening, cutting through the air and swishing about in chaos. And like a drain sucks down water, the hole in the wall made an escape for them, each one fleeing away in both complete verbal silence and ear-piercing volume of movement.

What was left was a mere shell of what had been. It was something that looked more like a man, symmetrical in design, but not yet something I would call beautiful. It had been emptied, but not yet filled.

"They have decided." The hollow man-like creature said.

"So they have. Let us go. We will come back for them later." Joshua said.

We turned away from the back of cell and walked out. Joshua turned left, back towards the stairs that now climbed up and out of sight.

As we started walking towards the stairs, something pulled on the inside of me. I felt particularly drawn towards one of the doors on my right, opposite of the man's cell that had its door ripped off.

"Joshua, wait a sec." I said.

Joshua turned around and looked at me as I gazed at the door in front of me. He smiled.

"Scythe, do you know who is in there?"

"No. I just felt like...."

"Like you want to get in there?" He asked.

"Yes." I said.

"I am proud of you. Go for it."

I did as I saw Him do before, and stood on my tip-toes, calling through the little window.

"Hello?"

"Yes? What do you want?" A man's voice shot back.

"Don't you want to get out of there?"

"Of course I do you daft idiot! But one can't just strut about after doing what I have done!" The man countered.

"As I understand it, you can come out if you like." I said.

"I may be able to come out, but I won't be able to *stay* out unless..."

I waited for him to finish but he never did. I could hear him sobbing inside, and it didn't sound like he was going to conclude his thought.

"Unless what?" asked the being behind me that Joshua had just led out of the hole.

"Unless I talk to the man I wronged and beg forgiveness from him. Until then I deserve to be here. I may be able to leave at points, but I find myself wandering right back and locking myself in because of what I have done. I deserve this punishment."

"Who do you need to talk to so badly?" the being asked.

"A Man named Joshua." He said quietly.

"Wait a sec. Joe? Is that you?" I asked, bewildered. I had met Joe not long before coming to The Abode. He was one of the most dislikable people I had ever met in life, and had even tried killing Joshua on more than one occasion.

Joshua ran up to the door, and I stepped aside as He stuck His face into the gap in the door.

"Joe. I am here. What do you want to tell Me? "

Joe did not hesitate. I heard him stand up and run to the door, their faces now inches apart.

"Joshua? You are here? Why are you here?" Joe asked.

"For the reason you hope. What do you want to tell me?"

"That I became what I preached! I preached fire and brimstone and it is where I ended up! I realize now it is not my doctrines or my theology that will save me. You are the deciding factor. I want to beg your forgiveness!"

There are times when a man cries, and there are times when he weeps. Weeping is the messy sort, involving runny noses and even the loss of control over saliva, with drool sometimes inadvertently running out of the mouth and down to the chin. This kind of brokenness is not attractive in a physical sense, but of the utmost value and attractiveness in every other sense. He was in utter disarray. It was disarmingly magnificent and beautiful.

"Open the door." Joshua said firmly.

"I can't! What I have done is too horrible!" Joe said with grief weighing heavy in his voice.

"Phalanx?" Joshua said to the being standing behind me that had just been emptied.

The creature's face twisted into surprise. "I haven't been called that in a long time."

"I know." Joshua said as He grinned.

Like it knew exactly what Joshua wanted, Phalanx walked up and looked into the cell as Joshua moved out of the way.

Phalanx spoke slowly and clearly. "What *you* have done is too horrible? Do not underestimate what He has done and do not so arrogantly elevate the power of your sin over the costly sacrifice He has made and the superior power therein. What you have done is nothing in comparison to the thousands of years of deception that I sowed into the earth, and what I did is nothing, I say *nothing*, compared to what He did. Put things into perspective."

I heard a click from the other side of the door, and it slowly opened. Joe stood there, a skinny comparison to what he was on earth. Joshua didn't hesitate for a moment. Leaping forward, Joshua wrapped Joe up in His arms, lifting him into the air.

"You are already forgiven. Now you must receive it. It is your choice." Joshua said.

Joe nodded, not being able to speak through the tears and choking of brokenness, and Joshua put him back down on the ground.

Joshua turned to us and said, "Some are here. Some are above. The difference between the two isn't primarily sin. The difference between the two is that some have accepted that they are forgiven while the other's haven't."

"Yet." I added, smiling.

"Exactly. And some haven't even recognized it yet, thus they need to be told. And still others don't need to recognize it for they already know it. But *all* must receive it. It is as simple as unwrapping a gift, as Joe can now attest to, but that doesn't mean it is always easy."

Joe smiled as he wiped his nose with the backside of his hand.

Two things became clear to me at this point. First was that Joshua wasn't just trying to save people, but He was going to restore certain fallen beings as well. This, I must record, did not appeal to me at the time, nor did I see the reason behind it. I had yet to understand the glorious mystery that *who* The Eternal is influences everything, not just certain things. Second was that Joshua had just used Phalanx to restore someone else, a creature that a few moments prior was lording over thousands of other fallen beings. These two realities brought me closer to the conclusion that Joshua's ability to make wonderful things out of awful situations was a characteristic about Him that I had obviously underemphasized.

Eighteen

Phalanx and Joe lead the way up the stairs. Because both were limping and at a loss of energy, what began as a jog to escape this place became a close crawl. Their slowing down gave me a moment to ask Joshua a few of the questions that had been lingering in my mind.

"Why does it seem that we were more effective here than we were in the Lands of Oblivion? Both subjects we approached decided to come."

"I wondered if you would ask about that. They are more desperate here, and less uncertain what reality is like outside of My grace. It isn't so much fog and shadows here but stark horror. In the Lands of Oblivion, their punishment is isolation. They are left to their own clouded thinking. This is, no doubt, awful. But down here in The Abyss, the punishment they inflict upon one another is much more overt. Did you see Phalanx's skin?"

"Yes. It looked like he had been whipped." I said.

"He had. It is not The Eternal that punishes people here for ever, it is the people and beings themselves."

"What do you mean?" I asked.

"Do you remember what Joe said? He said he deserved to be there in that cell. Those that live here are convinced that they must pay for what they did in life.

They *want* to be punished. Every person and creature, when they pass from the realm of the earth to the next, instinctively knows their shortcomings in life. The judgement is more of a realm of truth than anything else. You see things as they are. Nothing can be hidden, good or bad. Everything is brought to light and made conscious. They become immediately aware of justice and what it would take for them to right their wrongs. And because those here won't receive what I did, they go about trying to right the scales of justice on their own."

"But how? Nothing they do can pay for anything they did. It is a useless endeavor, isn't it?"

"It is. But they are convinced, just as men were throughout the ages in every culture and religion, that they can punish themselves and it will make a difference. There is an inherent awareness in men of their shortcoming. Thus, they make insufficient attempts to pay for what they have done. Some called it penance. Sacrifice. Holy suffering. Mortification. Chastisement. Others think of it as a tangible, verifiable, form of repentance. Thus, Phalanx's scars."

"Do you mean that he did that to himself?"

Phalanx had been listening, and now spoke. "Not always. It is much more intense than that. There were many times when I would let others into my cell to do it for me."

"So you would whip yourself, because you felt guilty, but you also invited others to punish you as well?"

"Yes."

"That is sick." I said, the words slipping out before I thought them through. Phalanx didn't seem to disagree.

"That is all The Abyss is about. Punishment. We punish ourselves and each other. Everyone there wants it that way. The more extreme, the better."

"I don't get it. That is so twisted!" I said.

"It is." said Joshua. "But it isn't that far-fetched if you think of life without the cross. Someone has to pay. Someone has to right the scales. Their destruction of one another gives them the fleeting sense that their wrongs have been paid for. Thus, they praise one another for the harm they rain down on each other. Each individual there invites everyone else to degrade and maim them. It is what life looks like without Me."

"So what determines if they go to The Lands of Oblivion or to The Abyss? Or even deeper?"

Joshua smiled. "Good question. Catholicism liked to order sins according to their seriousness, from venial to mortal. The Eternal does not view sin in this way. To Him, sin is sin. Murder and telling a white lie are both the same amount of an infraction. Either way, men need someone to pay for their wrongs. Thus, men aren't sent to a specific level of this horrid world according to how evil their acts were in life. All are equally lost apart from Me. But, that does not mean that the severity of their sins does not in any way play a part in determining where they end up."

"So, what they did *does* influence where they end up? I thought you just said it doesn't." I asked.

"It doesn't influence the Eternal's judgement. It *does* influence their own judgement upon themselves."

"How so?" I asked.

"What determines where they end up is not how bad they were in life or the severity of their sin, but how much punishment they feel they must inflict upon themselves in order for their wrongs to be made right. The greater the sin doesn't necessarily mean the deeper the plane they inhabit, but it does mean that it is a greater debt of guilt that must be carried, which *can* result in the person or creature demanding that they live in a more harsh, horrible place. To them, the thought of going to

The Abode is completely out of the question. That is nothing short of absurd to them, for the reality of one's shortcoming is something everyone becomes aware of when they move from the earth to this side. As I said, everything is brought into the light, flayed and left open, with all to see. Nothing is hidden anymore. "

"I am not sure I follow." I said.

"Ok. Let me give you an example. A thief of diamonds may feel that the punishment he would receive by living in the Lands of Oblivion suits the crime, while an abortionist may realize that the Lands of Oblivion is far too lenient a punishment for the innocent lives he has taken.

Let me pause and make it clear: The Eternal is not making the call. He is so empowering and trusting that He even allows men to decide where they go, though He desires that none shall perish. His judgment of all men is summated in My sacrifice. It ends there. Judgement is more about seeing things as they are than anything else. What men do when that moment arrives is up to them. The Eternal tells men not to sin not because He will judge them if they do, but because He knows that sin harms them and He deeply cares for their well being. He knows that inevitably, men will judge themselves for the very things He said not to partake in.

Here is the point, Scythe; Men did horrible things in their lives but I do not determine the punishment they succumb to. I determine their salvation out of it. I determine their reward for what they did right, not their punishment for what they did wrong. They determine their punishment themselves, and they are very "fair" or "just" or "right" in their judgement, at least, according to the standards of justice.

Nonetheless, I do not agree with their judgements and self-inflictions. I do not agree with ignoring and rejecting the cross. Receiving grace is the only humble response to sin. Getting what you do not deserve is the only low road, the only way of the meek, and the only right response to my sacrifice. Anything else, while appearing to be noble, is evil in its most raw state."

Joshua sighed. "Long story short, they choose to be here and wallow in punishment for what they did rather than accept that all of their wrongs and trespasses have been paid in full. The real test of a person's or creature's ability to receive the cross takes place when they stumble. If they wallow in condemnation, guilt, and shame, groveling in the dirt and agonizing over their sin, then they are rejecting the cross, dishonoring it by trying to pay for their deeds with their own self inflicted punishment. But, if they quickly get back up and receive grace, the very thing they do not feel worthy of receiving, they honor the cross. Whether it be internal guilt or more extreme external forms, punishing oneself does nothing to honor The Eternal, but receiving grace when you don't deserve it is one of the highest ways to honor My costly sacrifice upon the cross. Everything has been paid for, if they would only humble themselves, and reach out and receive what they do not deserve."

"I did!" Joe said, wheezing as he slowly took another step upwards.

"Yes you did, Joe." Joshua said, then turned to me and loudly said, "Took him awhile didn't it?", as He gently elbowed me in the side and winked.

"Yeah, yeah, yeah." Joe rolled his eyes, smiling. "Religion does that. I was so unaware of my double standards. Being down there," he pointed back in the direction of his cell, "made me realize that You were the only one to love me in all of my legalism and hatred."

Joshua responded by smiling as He put His arm around Joe, helping him up the next step.

"Do you remember," Joshua said slowly, "when you tried to kill me with that knife?"

Everyone started laughing. The ridiculousness of trying to kill Joshua was humorous. Nobody could take His life. That was the impossibility of impossibilities. Even before, nobody took His life: He laid it down. The thought of Joe with his knife was pathetic, and Phalanx must have thought so as well, for he let loose the most beautiful laugh, sounding like the water of a summer stream as it fell and rose over boulders in its path. The sounds he expelled confirmed that he was altogether not human. I had a feeling that his beauty was not far from being unveiled, and like Valerie had changed when she got near the light of the Abode, I figured Phalanx would likely follow the same pattern.

The moment of laughter seemed to strengthen Joe and Phalanx, and we gained speed again. Every once in awhile they would slow down again, due to the lack of sleep, light, and true air. I would notice Joshua softly touch some part of their body; their back, hand, or shoulder, and they would instantly gain speed again. At first I thought He was reminding them to keep up a greater speed, but then I realized that He was imparting strength to them every time He touched them. He knew that without His touch they could never make it out of those depths.

We passed through the black wall at the top of our climb and into the shanty town of the Lands of Oblivion. I saw Cecilia outside of her house, still digging in the dirt at an attempt to cajole her beans to life, an endless and impossible endeavor. My heart went out to her. Joshua picked up on this and laid His hand on my shoulder.

"We will come back for her soon." He said gently, comforting my heart.

I didn't know Cecelia well, and I cared for her. I thought about how broken Joshua's heart must be over her, for He had know her forever, even woven the strands of her being together in the womb. I couldn't imagine the pain it caused Him to see someone He so dearly loved living that way.

After quite a time on the trail the light crept up on us like dawn. I watched as Joe and Phalanx started to take in deep breaths of air, like their lung capacity was expanding by the second. The whitish gray hue of Joe's skin turned pink, the way a heroin addict's color returns after a few weeks of detox. Phalanx's covering (as I am not sure if it was skin), stayed the same color, scars and all, and jet black.

We made it to the thicket of shame at the entrance, and Joshua and I took out our swords to clear the path once again. Both Joe and Phalanx jumped back when we unsheathed the swords, as though we had brought them all of this way to do some wicked thing to them. Joshua and I started laughing, and Joe and Phalanx calmed, walking back to us.

"Still a bit jumpy when we see weapons. Sorry about that. May take some time to get used to things up here." Phalanx said.

Though light was just on the other side of the mass of foliage, it effectively blocked out a majority of the brightness, leaving us still standing in darkness. Joshua and I started to hack away at the green, and soon had made a hole large enough for Joe to stick His head through and take his first look at The Abode. I didn't have to cease at swinging at the plants while he head was poked through the hole, as the sword would only cut that which I wanted it to. It looked like I was about to decapitate someone in the stocks, but the sword was totally harmless to Joe, and the thicket around him fell at his feet, significantly enlarging the hole, causing the radiance of the brightness on the other side to spill onto us.

Then suddenly, there was a scream that erupted behind me. I dropped the sword in fright, thinking that on the backswing I may have wounded Phalanx. Maybe the sword was only harmless to humans rather than Phalanx's kind.

I looked to see that Phalanx was standing clear of my swings, probably 8 feet away, and knew that it was not my sword that caused him to scream; something else caused him to. Phalanx was levitating a foot or so off the ground, his arms extended, and his face was looking directly upwards. He seemed to be in the most excruciating pain. His screaming was consistent, continuing until it ceased for the brief moment when he would gather another lung-full of breath, then would and start again.

"Joshua, is he ok?" I yelled loud enough so that Joshua could hear me over Phalanx.

"Yes!" Joshua shouted back.

But Phalanx kept screaming. I wanted to help him but felt powerless because I didn't know how to. It was the same feeling I had the day my sister gave birth to my nephew. She screamed and screamed and there was nothing I could do. Did I need to pull Phalanx out of the air? What was causing him the pain?

Then as I watched, Phalanx's black skin broke open in various places on his body. It looked extremely painful. Every place where his skin split, a fiery light shown through. The splits enlarged and increased in number, until most of his body was lacerated in this way. Phalanx now started struggling, whipping his head back and forth, as though he was resisting whatever was taking place. Then, like a child tears a piece of paper, Phalanx's black skin was viciously torn apart. It fell to the ground slowly, like ash from a fire, and Phalanx settled to the ground.

"Welcome back." Joshua said calmly.

"Thank you." The voice echoed back, now even deeper than before, the reverberation shaking the clothes on my body with its resonance.

Phalanx now stood before us without a shred of black layered upon him. In fact, he was exactly the opposite of black. He wasn't just white, but a shining white, bright with radiance. He stood at a height of nine feet at least, wore a gold sarong that covered down to his thighs, leaving his chest bare. He was extremely muscular. Thick gold bands encircled his arms above his biceps, and his blonde hair hung down to his shoulders. He looked like what I imagined Thor would look like on steroids. I was glad he liked me, because he wasn't someone you would want on the other team.

"Why were you screaming like that?" I asked intensely, still shaken up from Phalanx's sounds.

"It wasn't pain that caused me to scream. It was pleasure. After being accustomed to pain for so long, pleasure is more of a shock than more pain is. I was screaming because light, this light, was bringing me to life again."

"Like a snake sheds its skin and becomes a new creation," Joshua said, "So did he shed the skin that he had wrapped himself in for so long. He was just born anew."

"I had been warned by others below that the fires there are simply an imitation of the fire here." Phalanx said. "The fire here is much stronger than what we have down there. Below, they use that counterfeit fire for punishment and pain, but here fire refines. The light here burned away my old covering, and it is *that* burning that truly terrifies those below. It is the goodness of the Eternal that causes us to tremble. It is light of life and the flame of love that causes the greatest pleasure and thus, the greatest horror to those hiding in darkness. It mercilessly burns past shame and unveils its all-encompassing acceptance."

I still didn't think he needed to scream like that, and after looking at Phalanx in both wonder and slight irritation, I shrugged and walked through the thicket and into The Abode.

Nineteen

"This way." Joshua said as we passed the banqueting hall in The Abode that I had eaten in and seen Rachel. "It is time to reinstate Phalanx."

We had been walking for some time, and when we entered into the City, the people walking the streets would see us, stand still and stare, then break into applause towards Joshua. I began to get the feeling that Phalanx was a bigger deal than I knew.

"Who is this guy?" Joe said, pointing at Phalanx's back as we followed behind him and Joshua. Unsure, I shrugged.

We rounded a corner and came upon a looming building made of stone. Joshua pushed open the double doors and led us inside, walking to the center of the room.

The room was circular with marble floors, and twelve seats were distributed around the circumference of the room. Settled in the seats that encircled us were men and creatures that looked young but had a curious look of ancientness in their eyes, as though they had looked upon many eras. One man with a scar on his neck spoke, the moving of his mouth barely discernible beneath the thickness of his white beard.

"Hello Joshua."

"Hello Mark. Good to see you again."

"You as well, sire. Thank you for bringing him. We will handle it from here."

"Thank you. Phalanx, they will care for you for now. I have other business to attend to."

"Joshua." Phalanx said.

"Yes, my friend?"

"Thank you. You are a most gracious King."

"You are most welcome. It is very good to have you here again. Lets stay here this time, eh?" Joshua grinned, turned and led Joe and I out of the room.

After we got outside the double doors, I asked, "Who were those guys?"

"They are the counsel assigned to reinstate Phalanx."

"Reinstate him to what?"

"To power" Joshua said as we rounded the corner, heading back in the direction of the banqueting hall.

"You didn't already reinstate him to power? The change he underwent right before we passed the thicket seemed to be quite a change to me." I said.

"It was quite a change, wasn't it? As far as Phalanx and I go, we are clear. But that doesn't mean that everything is sorted out just yet." Joshua said.

"How so?"

"Power comes from right relationship, and while I have forgiven him and thus redeemed him, those that he wronged in his life still need the opportunity to pardon what he did. Power here is always understood in the context of community. Restoration is instant with Me, but it takes time in the context of relationship with others. One could say that vertically, Phalanx is fine. But horizontally, there is much mending that needs to be made. In other words, I have forgotten the mess he has made, but that doesn't negate that it still needs to be cleaned up.

That is the purpose of the counsel. They are wise in relational matters and will walk him through who he needs to talk with and receive grace from. The result is that Phalanx will feel accepted here, even trusted and thus empowered, despite what he did. The goal is to restore Phalanx to the fullness of what he used to be, and that can't happen until those he harmed come before him and are reconciled to him in fullness. As others impart grace to him, shame over what he did will be erased, thus naturally reinstating him to power again. Some wounds are healed by other humans rather than The Eternal Himself, because they took place in the context of humanity rather than Divinity. Fortunately for Phalanx, everyone here has longed to tell him that they forgive him for what he has done. They excitedly await for the moment they get to lavish the priceless commodity of grace upon him.

In fact, they think upon that moment of forgiveness with the same passion that a father on earth yearned for the moment of murderous revenge towards the man that killed his daughter. Now wait a moment; hear Me out. Of course, here a wholly different heart is behind it, but revenge is still a reality in this realm. The difference is the way one takes their revenge. Before, men would inflict revenge by taking another's life or slandering someone's name. It was barbaric. Here, revenge can only look like goodness and grace. It is the epitome of heaping burning coals, yet not with the hope of a painful or embarrassing searing, but the burning away of shame and guilt.

Revenge on this side is more wild and wonderful than before; the sort that leaps up and instantly goes for the jugular. Forgiveness is the only flavor of revenge that satisfies the appetites of men in these lands. They are too wise to think that anything else would provide them sustenance."

Joe nodded. "Its taken a while to come to terms with it, but I have come to learn that *real* justice is grace. Anything less is hypocrisy."

I was surprised at this statement, considering Joe's background and past inability to give grace or receive it, but I was learning that it is sometimes those that are most religious that make the best examples of grace. He was learning very quickly. *"Quicker than me!"* I thought to myself.

We were now quite a ways from the circular room, and nearing the banqueting hall. Passing many buildings, I entertained ideas of what they were intended for and what went on within their walls. I had only seen the insides of a few of the many buildings in the City on this level, and what I had seen was beautiful. I yearned to see more.

Maybe a block away from the building that had the banqueting hall inside, Joshua turned abruptly to the right and faced a little concave in the side of the building next to us. Above the steps that led downwards and into what looked like the bottom of the building was wood a sign whose intricately carved letters read, "The Cellar".

"One of my favorite places. We need rest. Come." Joshua said as He slowly stepped downwards and made His way under the hanging sign.

I began to hear the sounds before I ever pushed open the saloon style doors down in the bowels of that building. We had walked down a flight of old stairs, diving down and plaining out into a enormous cellar. The walls, which were hundreds of yards from each other, were composed of stone, and rather than sharp ninety degree angles between the walls and ceiling, the walls and ceiling melded together in a spheroidal way, making more of arch for a ceiling than a flat surface above us. Though the room was large, it had a coziness about it that invited me in to its warmth.

People were seated at wooden tables all throughout the room, every individual with a drink in front of them, and short little men-like creatures were running about, refilling the glasses from spigots on huge wooden barrels that were propped up on their sides all along the edges of the room.

There were also large stone troughs, standing about four feet off of the ground, and filled with wood fires that just by looking at it made you feel safe and peaceful, as though you had just come inside from the cold and now had the subtle joy of warming yourself by the flames. The fires burned not just in white, yellow, and orange, but every color, resembling Jacob's coat.

Laughter filled the air. It was not the place for a quiet conversation, but the kind of place where you could come inside with muddy boots and not feel the need to take them off upon entry. If a person had guard, it was let down effortlessly here. This was a place of peace, but not of the kind that comes with silence, but the type that only comes in an atmosphere where anything goes.

Joshua sat down at a nearby table, and people at the surrounding table immediately stood and applauded Him. He graciously nodded, acknowledging and accepting their praise, then turned to the small, chubby little man with golden hair and wearing an apron standing next to us that was awaiting His order.

"We will have the strongest stuff you've got." Joshua said.

Moments later, large steins with a shimmering liquid arrived, and Joshua didn't hesitate. He downed the pint or so of drink immediately, slammed the mug down, and off and running was the little man again to refill it.

"Try it! It is wonderful. We started this batch long before the earth was constructed. After all, it isn't just a *place* I went to prepare for you!"

"I'll drink to that." Joe said, and knocked back the liquid. "My God! That *is* incredible, isn't it?"

Joe and Joshua then started laughing for no explainable reason. I had the sudden feeling of being left behind, with a ever increasing sense that I wanted to catch up. So down went the beverage.

The taste was unimaginable. It felt like taste buds that I never knew existed fired off with incredible speed and strength, for tastes that aren't comparable to anything I had eaten before overtook my mouth. It felt like I was tasting a thousand gustatory delights at one time, each distinct and searing itself into the memories of my tongue. When it hit my stomach, it swirled about, like it was alive and wanted to give its life to me. I could literally feel thoughts and feelings about The Eternal being unlocked in me. I understood mysteries. I felt the essence of freedom bear down on me, ushering me into liberty of the heart that I hadn't fathomed before. I had no reason to hold back thoughts or feelings as I was more confident than ever that even if I was misled in them, I would be accepted. I felt bold, even invincible.

I didn't take my lips off the side of the mug, continuing to chug. I only came up for air once the last drop slid down the glass and into my mouth.

"Wow! What was that?" I blurted out. I realized I said it loud enough for everyone at the tables near us to hear, but nobody turned and looked.

"The private reserves of private reserves. After all, this stuff was made back when it was just Us," Joshua said as the edge of His mouth lifted up into a half and hidden smile like He had a secret.

"By 'us', You mean just You, The Eternal, and The Matchmaker?" Joe asked.

"Yep. We made it for each other. Back in those days...*That* is what you'd call a party. Wow."

"Yeah, but what do You call it?" I said, again a bit too loud for normal conversation.

"I call it Matchmaker. Liquid form. Others call it The Spirit of spirits or the spirit of burning. Can you feel it down inside?"

"You bet I can! Another!" I called out. A little pudgy man was at my side instantly, shuffling away my empty glass. Moments later, another stein was sitting in front of me, luring me with its gleaming surface. Like a soap bubble's surface can encompass every color in the rainbow, so did the surface of this drink.

"But, it seems You are all we need, or should need. Why should we resort to something other than You alone, Joshua?" Joe asked. I thought it was a very insightful question, and this time I had the answer.

"I suppose someone could make that argument about the light here too then." I said. "This isn't being filled with something other than Him. Everything here is Him. This isn't in addition to Him; This *is* Him. From what I have picked up, everything in these lands is possessed by Him."

"True." said Joshua. "Do not hold back. Drink your fill. You are in need of rest. Enter into it."

"Rest? Like sleep? Will this drink cause us to slumber?" Joe asked.

"Rest isn't specifically physical, and doesn't only come by sleep, though sleep comes easily here. Rather, rest is simply partaking of joy."

"Rest is...joy?" Joe said, slightly confused.

"Yes. Rest takes place in the context of happiness. One can work, but if it is joyful work, it can be restful.

Joy comes in many different forms, but this is one of my favorite types." said Joshua.

I lost count how many times the little man came back to refill our mugs. With each additional drink, my mind became more clarified in matters pertaining to Joshua and The Eternal, and less clear with everything that would distract me from the former. During this time Joe, Joshua, and I spoke of realities more deep than the ocean and higher than the sky. To someone that has not prepped themselves with near marination as we had, what escaped from our mouths would sound only like idealism and far-fetched impracticalities. But for us, in this mindset of such clarity, faith, and boldness, reality could be nothing short of such greatness.

I do not recall at what point it happened, but I remember a distinct shift in the conversation where Joshua began to speak directly to Joe or myself, and would lavish us with affirmation. He would go on for twenty minutes or so, locking eyes with one of us, and would say the very things that we desperately needed to hear but did not know we needed to hear. He knew the secrets of our hearts; our dreams, our desires, our needs. Like a skilled surgeon, He would flay our heart open, only to revel in how much He adored it. He brought to light the most hidden places, then would spread His complete acceptance, understanding, and affection to it. It was incredibly revealing, but safe. If anyone else had done it, it would have been an intrusion. But when Joshua did it, one couldn't help but crumple into tears. His words answered questions I never knew I had and questioned answers I thought I had a grasp on; answers I had come up with on my own that were unloving towards myself. He embraced and affirmed every detail about me.

I liked myself more after being with Joshua.

Many think that in these lands we only spend our time praising Him. This is not true. Much of the time, one is intensely humbled by the very opposite. Most assuredly, there is nothing more humbling. The mark of a true king is always that he uses his power to serve those around him rather than lording it over them. Thus, Joshua proved to be the King of kings time and time again. He never failed to serve others before we could get the chance to beat Him to it, and He was always the first to extend love. He demonstrated His royalty by being the first to go low. His humility made us humble. His stooping low brought us to our knees. It was the fact that He was seated so high above all else and yet acted as He did that causes us extreme wonder.

Do not mistake me; It is not that we do not praise Him. Every movement one makes here is praise. One cannot function outside of it. Rather than an action or choice, it is a ever present reality. Every step, every breath, every blink of the eye is filled with the awe and wonder of The Eternal. The one impossibility in these lands was to do something that *wasn't* praise. And that may not come as a surprise, but what was even more astonishing to me was that He also loved to exalt us as well; that He spent His time finding glorious intricacies about each of us and making them known. He is not One to be out given.

After what seemed like a lifetime of laughter and affirmation, Joshua stood and walked towards the stairs to leave. As He did, every person in the room stood and applauded Him. Joshua bowed slightly, acknowledging their honor, then turned to the stairs. We followed Him out of the stone room and back up the stairs.

Twenty

It had been day when we had entered The Cellar, and I assumed that it would be night when we exited. It was not. One does not typically leave an establishment such as The Cellar in the brightness of noonday but rather at dusk or in the dark of night, and despite the many hours we had stayed there, that is exactly the state outside when we exited. I had forgotten that night was no longer, and that day and light was all I would ever know again. Even in shutting my eyes light would still make its way into me.

Joshua took us to the neighborhoods where the mansions lined the streets and walked each of us to the door of our own abode. I was not surprised to find that the uninhabited mansion next to my own was now filled. It was very like Joshua to put two people that were enemies in our past life together in this one. Joe waved to me as he walked into his mansion, and I waved back as I pushed open the door to my own that sat next door.

"Get some rest. I'll see you soon." Joshua said.

I said goodbye to Joshua, and stepped inside. The interior, which I was curious to explore, was extravagant but simple. At first I was taken back by this, but soon it became clear that Da Vinci was right; Simplicity *is* the ultimate sophistication. The entry room had very little decorating it, yet did not feel empty or cold but inviting.

Only a few pictures hung on the walls, leaving them feeling uncluttered and clear. I removed my shoes, which I was still wearing from my entry into The Abode, and realized that I had no need for them anymore. Shoes protected the feet, and my feet were not longer under threat. I expected the white floor (that seemed to be marble) to feel cold as I stepped upon it, but it was warm like skin, touching me back. It was then that I first entertained the idea that this house may be more than just a house.

The entry room was rectangular, with the door I had just walked through at one end and two hallways branching off to the left and to the right on the far side of the room, making a "T" intersection. On the wall that faced me across the room, the wall that one has to walk towards and look at if they are going to enter into the rest of the house, hung a large mirror. It was the first mirror I had seen since I had left the earth.

I slowly made myself across the room, curious as to what the mirror would behold. The closer I got, the more surprised I was.

I was a younger version of myself. All wrinkles were gone from my face, and though I could tell it was me, the person I looked at in the mirror was clearly more beautiful than the person I had seen in the mirror on earth. The odd thing about it is that I couldn't determine any actual stark physical changes besides the fact that I looked younger. In other words, it wasn't as though my nose, which I had always felt was a bit too big, was any smaller. It wasn't that I had changed in physical ways that made me beautiful, it was that something of the spirit had changed about me, something that washed over everything else in the body and soul. I realized that while the physical is the most tangible, it is not the most real. The spiritual had glazed over everything, changing all of me. In fact, I had not changed but had been made something altogether new. The old of me was not comparable to the new. I was majestic.

I found myself shying away from the mirror, worried for a moment that I would stare at myself forever, hooked on the beauty that I beheld coming forth from my own being. I was concerned that I would take my focus off of Him and put it on myself. I remembered verses about men worshipping angels and shuttered at the thought of such a compromise.

I now stood a few feet away from the mirror, looking down at the white floor. I realized in that moment that I had a choice; To cower away from the beauty of who I was now, and try to avoid it through false humility and fear, or I realized, I could embrace who I was. I could remember that it was Joshua that had made me this way, and that every time I saw my own beauty, it was a reflection of His.

I whipped my head back up, holding it high, not in pride but as an act that was defiant to it, and looked into the mirror again. This time instead of concern I felt heat rush up inside my chest and make its way to my eyes, which started to bleed tears of gratitude. I felt my heart connect with reality. Peace, a version of peace that only comes when a person has been humbled in spirit, leapt upon me. I stood there looking at myself, silently weeping. Tears dripped off my face and splattered to the ground. This was my offering. This was my worship.

He was beautiful. I knew it more in that moment than ever before.

I wasn't sure what Joshua had meant by "get some rest", as I never felt myself grow tired anymore, but decided to try to sleep anyways. I didn't know where my bedroom was located, so I walked to the right of the mirror after taking one more look at the glory that rested upon me.

The hallway led into a large, open room. Once I got inside I realized that both going to the left or the right at the mirror would bring a person into the same area, just on different sides of the wall on which the mirror hung. The room was spacious, so large that it would take me a minute to walk across it from end to end. The back wall, furthest from the front door, was barely a wall at all since it was completely transparent, revealing what I would assume was my back yard, though it stretched out as far as my eyes could see. From the quick glance that I made outside, a large, colorful garden was in bloom. Behind the garden were rolling hills of green, scattered with animals, some I had seen before like eagles, horses, and lions, but many that I couldn't recall from my previous life. Rivers cut through the hills, some ending in waterfalls that plunged down from great heights and ending in large, crystal pools of water.

I was bombarded with all of the details of the room and the yard outback, but the thing that most caught my attention was the fact that I was not alone. Surprisingly, a man wearing a black suit stood on one end of the room, his arms at his side. He was looking at me pleasantly, like he was waiting for something.

"Can I help you?" I asked.

"No of course not. That is my job!" He said happily.

"Excuse me, do I know you?" I said.

"You should. I am your butler. My name is Joie."

"Nice to meet you, Joie. I am..."

"...Scythe. I know!"

"And you know my name how?" I asked.

"I have been assigned to you for many years. Since you were conceived."

"But we never had a butler in my family on earth."

"I know. My role was more unseen then, but of the same nature. I am here to help you in any way that I can. I am at your service."

"Well, thank you." I said awkwardly, not knowing how to interact with someone whose job it was to serve me.

Joie must have noticed. "Don't let it be odd, sir. The only difference between now and then is that you can see me now. I have always been around. It was my job to protect you, to minister to you, to fight for you, and even to play with you, though I must say that you stopped wanting to play as you got older."

"How could I play with you when I was little if I couldn't see you?"

"Play is not dictated by sight, but by the weightlessness of the heart. I tickled you and you would laugh. We would race through mustard fields as your dog ran along side us." Joie paused, smiling. "You always won."

I didn't say it out loud, but he was right. As a child I had felt the presence of someone; someone unseen, but someone pleasant and safe. I didn't know who they were, but I knew they were good. There were times when I would have the irresistible notion to laugh for no reason, like some invisible thing was tickling me. Joy doesn't need a purpose to work its magic, for joy is purpose in and of itself.

"Well Joie, it is nice to finally meet you."

"Yes, it is. It has been a long time coming. I have waited for this moment for a very long time."

I liked him. He was familiar to me, which gave me the sense of comfort. As odd as it sounds, he didn't feel like a butler to me as much as a brother.

"So, what is out there, past the glass?" I asked.

"Glass? Ah, you mean the diamond. That is your garden and beyond that, whatever you want."

"Diamond?"

"Yes. We know how to form it here. The window is made of pure and perfect diamond. All of the wealth of the earth could not pay for that single piece of your house."

The "window" stood at least fifty feet tall, and thousands of feet wide, spanning the entirety of the room.

"And what did you mean by 'whatever you want?'"

"Well, as you have already learned, The Countries of Matrimony stretch as far up as one desires to go. They also go as far wide as one desires. What you are starting to grasp is that there are no boundaries on this land. It is the same, in a different way, with your back yard. Do you see those flowers in your garden?"

Joie pointed to a specific plant that was displaying large, orange and blood-red flowers. The colors were moving about on the surface of the flower rather than staying put like I was used to.

"Yes."

"Give me a second. I need a moment to think of how to explain this. Ah, yes. You see, just as this place is as high and wide as one could ever go, it is also infinite in detail, so one can go in and in just as he can go out or up."

"I'm not sure I follow." I said.

"Understandably. It is a bit much for a new mind to grasp. Say a person were to take that flower up in their hand and look into it. If one wanted, they could get lost in the world that is in that flower forever. By 'in and in' I mean that every thing here possesses depths that one can stumble into and never find the end of. There are worlds upon worlds here. And that is just within one flower. "

"Overload." I said blandly.

"Yes, that is to be expected. Beauty," Joie beamed, "is infinitely layered in The Countries of Matrimony. You can take a million years to peel back one layer to find the next to be even more glorious and breathtaking than the last."

I didn't have much to say, as there comes a point when one has been constantly barraged with surprise and awe where you cease to react, and all one can do is shrug. It isn't meant to be disrespectful, but the inevitable result of being inundated.

"I don't mean to overwhelm you, but I haven't answered your question yet. You asked me what I meant by 'whatever you want'. Do you still want to know?"

"Yes. I think so!" I sputtered out amidst laughter, snapping out of my transfixed state.

Joie smiled. "Just as there are many worlds to be explored and discovered up and out and in, The Eternal also has given you a place to create and discover whatever you want, there beyond your garden. It is a place set aside to create a whole world of your own, just as you like it, and like the flower and the whole of The Countries of Matrimony, it will have no limits. You will be able to go into it as far as you want, out as far as you wish, and up as high as you can dream. The earth that you used to live on, or even the galaxy that earth hung in, will not match the size of the world that will be upon one blade of grass in the place you will conjure up."

"I think I need a nap." I said pathetically. I meant to be more accommodating to this revelation, but I just didn't have it in me. A nap seemed like the only way I could escape from the besiegement of new thoughts and understanding. I wasn't tired necessarily, I just needed a bit of a break.

"Of course. Let me show you the way." Joie said.

Joie led me up a spiral staircase on the left side of the room. I wasn't paying attention to the details around me anymore, say, to what the staircase was made of or pondering how the banister was made so smooth, almost wet, but still dry and leaving no residue on my hand. I figured that I had all of eternity to discover more about my abode in the Abode, and right now all I wanted to discover was how a pillow felt on my cheek as I mentally checked out.

Joie had led me into a room and ushered me towards a bed. Moments later, I was tucked in. I felt weightless, like I wasn't laying down at all. I was covered in thick silky blankets and knew that I was in bed, but it felt like I was floating, with no pressing weight upon the part of my body that was on the mattress. Because of this, the moment I laid down I started to drift away.

Twenty One

The wobbling light that I had shuttered from had no effect on me. I walked towards it without thinking, the way one does when they have no concern for their own safety. I was a man driven.

The stairs dipped off so steeply that they were like a cliff. I was down them faster than falling, and suddenly at the bottom. The stench and heat were overwhelming, and I walked past a lake of sorts before seeing the door. It was as though I knew where to go though I had no idea where I was.

I did not knock. I kicked the door in, maybe from anger, maybe from love; I couldn't tell which.

A voice gurgled from the blackness.

"How are you here already? I am not expecting you. Get out! Unless of course, you want your insides spilled on this floor. I like either choice."

Fire bubbled up inside me, the way water boils over heat.

"I can come whenever I want. Now, while I talk with you, you cannot lie, and you must obey me. Do you understand?"

A voice came through a cry and scream, barely discernible, "Yesssssss!"

"Good. I am glad we understand each other. I have but one question. Do you want out?"

"Yes!" It hissed. "Do not tell! I beg you!"

"Then it is settled." I said.

* * *

I opened my eyes. The ceiling of my mansion shone back at me, like it had been waiting for my consciousness and was happy to see it returned. The light was all around me, almost dancing around me like it too had a consciousness. In the dream, the light was not of the same brand as here in the Abode, so this light caused me to give my attention to it again. I realized that even when I had my eyes shut, it still made it inside me, like my eye lids did nothing to seal it out. I covered my head with my blankets, thinking that I may be able to escape from it, not because I wanted to, but because I was curious to see how it acted. Play is one of the best ways of discovery. The light wasn't coming from a specific source at the moment, and seemed to be below the covers before I got there. I couldn't keep it out. Darkness may have filled the empty spaces in past lives, but in this world, light filled the voids. It hung in the atmosphere like air did.

I was refreshed in a different way upon waking. The cellar had somehow expanded my ability to retain new knowledge and joy, but sleep had been like a reset button for me. I still kept all that I had learned, but now felt impressionable again. I was ready for more.

"*The dream*" I thought. The dream had been quite dark, but it did not leave me feeling dark. I wasn't scared or drained by it. In fact, I felt as though I had been given some high-clearance information that wasn't usually doled out to the general public. I wasn't quite sure what the dream meant, where I was in the dream, or who was the owner of the diseased voice. I only knew that someone wanted out. Somewhere past the Abyss and the iron doors that lined its hallways, somewhere after that cliff of stairs bathed in that unstable glowing light, somewhere in the depths there was someone that wanted out.

"Good morning, sir." Joie stood in the doorway to the room I slept in.

"Hello!" I said loudly and happily.

"Would you care for some breakfast?"

"Sure. What do you have?"

"Anything you would like. Or I could make you something you have never tried."

I had always enjoyed trying new things, and here it was guaranteed to not disappoint.

"Throw something at me that I have never tried. The more unusual the better."

Joie chuckled. "Ok. You asked for it."

He turned and left the room. I got up and walked out of the bedroom, to the staircase I had climbed some time earlier.

"How long was I out?" I asked, as I watched Joie's back disappear down the spiral staircase.

"One could call it a few hours." He said.

"That is all? I felt like I slept for a few days."

"Time isn't the same here, nor is rest." Joie shouted out from below in a tone that clarified that he was reminding me of something that I should already know.

I was standing on a balcony that overlooked the large room. I looked up and saw that the staircase did not only spiral down, but up. One could get off at any floor they wanted.

"How many floors does it go up?" I said loudly, as Joie was still below me, walking to the other end of the large room with the window.

"Seven. But you can do with the house as you please."

I hurried downstairs and caught up with Joie.

"You mean I can rearrange the furniture?" I asked.

"Yes, of course. But you can do much more than that. The Eternal gave every son and daughter the authority to rearrange the way He created the earth. Remember that little tidbit about tossing mountains? If you could do that, surely you can order your house how you want it. Just speak to it and it will shift."

I stopped walking and Joie continue across the room. I was about a forth of the way across the large room and wanted to try out what Joie was talking about.

"I want a couch here." I said.

Immediately a beautiful, red couch that I had not noticed on the far end of the room moved by itself and positioned itself exactly where I had pointed.

"You can do better than that!" Hollered Joie, heckling me from some unknown location out of sight, probably another room.

"Ok, Fine. I want a wall here, tall and thick enough so I don't have to hear Joie critique me in skills I am just learning."

Immediately a tall wall appeared before me, sealing me off from the side of the house that Joie was in.

"Nevermind. I don't like it."

The wall vanished. As it disappeared I could hear Joie laughing in the other room from my ornery remark. He liked it. I was glad that he saw the humor in it rather than being hurt or offended by it. I was thankful that people, or at least Joie, understood my flavor of humor here.

Joie walked out from a room on the far side of the mansion. He was far away but he spoke rather than shouted, and I could hear him as clearly as if he was standing right next to me.

"This is what dominion looks like. This is what authority is. It all culminates in creativity. To be creative and thus, to have the ability to create is one of the greatest statements The Eternal makes about His love for you, for He has made you like Him."

"Yes, of course."

"You can design your whole house in this way. Do with it what you like; it is yours." Joie said.

Joie turned and started walking back towards the room he had just exited from, which I guessed was the kitchen.

I was entertaining ideas of how to decorate my house when a knock came from the front door, far away and behind the dividing wall that had the mirror on it.

It was Joshua. Something in my heart leapt when I opened the door and saw Him, as though hidden defibrillators resided in my chest and all they needed for an excuse to fire off was Joshua's nearness. His closeness was becoming more and more of an imperative to me, and my inner man gasped for Him like a drowned man gasps for air after surfacing.

"Hello Scythe. I trust you rested well?"

"Yes! And the house is brilliant!"

"We thought you would like it. Have you had a chance to go out back yet?"

"Into the field where the animals are?"

Joshua nodded.

"Not yet. I look forward to it. I got a bit sidetracked over the fact that I could do anything with the house that I see fit."

"Excellent. Well, do you mind if Joie makes us something to eat? Perhaps we could be off then."

"Not at all. Lets eat."

We walked into the large room where, on the far side of the room, Joie had set two places at a large wooden table. Every inch was covered in food with exception of the space that our empty plates and glasses took up. I sat down after Joshua did, and looked around in wonder at what was laid before me.

I was about to eat, then felt an old obligation to give thanks. I bowed my head and began to thank The Eternal for the meal. I was distracted from my daily ritual by Joshua's interruptive laughter.

"What?" I asked loudly, bringing my head up and looking at Joshua.

"If you have seen Me, you have seen the Eternal. If you want to say thanks, just say it to me! I am right here."

I began to smile, realizing how ridiculous it was to *pray* rather than to *talk* to Joshua. Prayer, after all, is talking with The Eternal. But if God is sitting with a person at the table and they "pray" rather than talk to Him, they aren't praying at all. When He is in the room and a person prays in a way that acts as though He is not, one has to wonder who they are talking to and if they are praying at all. I am not sure what they are doing at that point, maybe they are talking to themselves, but they surely aren't interacting with Him. It was humorous how religious I could still be, and how I was still learning what relationship looked like.

We ate, complimented Joie for his culinary skills, and were soon finished. We hadn't said much to each other, but now a question was looming in my mind.

"Where are we headed next?"

"Deeper."

"But..."

"No." He said firmly, cutting off my thought. "You are ready."

I was one to make my opinion and feelings known, especially with Joshua (and He always gave me the impression that He invited my thoughts), but I knew that if He was telling me that I was ready, then I was ready, despite the hesitations that I perceived in my own heart. I didn't feel pressured or forced into it; He simply knew something about me that I did not yet know. And because I knew that He knew me better than I knew myself, the decision to trust Him wasn't a hard one to make.

"Is anyone else going with us?"

"No, not this time."

"Do you have a specific target in mind?"

"I do."

"Who is it?"

"He is the owner of the gurgling voice you heard while in the realm of dreams."

"Ah! You know about that. But who is it?" I said.

"His name is Lucem Ferre."

"I have never heard of him before."

"Oh yes you have."

As always, Joshua smiled like He had a secret, then got up and walked out of my mansion. His smile told me that what He knew was a secret, but not one that He was hiding away.

I would soon discover that what Joshua knew was a secret that has been revealed to all, and thus not a secret in the least bit, at least not in the traditional sense. It is a hidden thing that only those that are searching find. It is a feast that only the hungry procure and a fountain that only the thirsty find and drink from. It was something that all could have if they would only search out a matter. It was something I had quietly entertained in the deepest recesses of my heart, but never made known before men. It is how this story ends, but more importantly and probably more accurately, how the real story all begins.

Twenty Two

It felt much shorter this time, the journey into the depths almost *smaller* somehow. We were already down the stairs to the long, grotesque hallway, lined with the metal doors of self imposed imprisonment. I could hear howling and cries, and knew that there were still many there, locked behind doors.

Joshua did not slow down as we walked past the cells, making His way directly towards the faded light at the end of the stretch.

Soon we were upon it. The hallway ended abruptly, ending in a cliff that plummeted downward. Joshua sat with His legs dangling over the edge, then turned Himself around, facing the ledge, and started to let himself down slowly, grasping small handholds on the face of the cliff or wedging His hand into small cracks in the rock. The drop was well over hundreds of feet, and the bottom floor, to which I supposed He was headed, shone red like it was aglow with some ungodly source of power. The fall alone threatened my peace, let alone the feeling I got from the light. Nonetheless, I figured if I fell Joshua could catch me, and I reasoned that I would rather be standing next to Him in that bloody light than anywhere in The Countries without Him. So I lowered myself down and began to climb.

Some of the holds only left enough room for one or two of my fingers, and just the tips of those fingers at that. Maybe it was because of the strength that my body had taken in from the light and drink of The Abode and the Cellar, but somehow I could easily support all of my weight with just the tip of just one of my fingers barely holding to a small lip of a rock jettisoning out from the wall. More and more boldness came over me, and soon I was swinging from one hold to the next, Joshua laughing below me as He looked up at my decent.

"Want to race?" He yelled up to me.

I felt invincible.

"Yes!"

And with that I let go completely. I saw Joshua rush past me as I plummeted past Him, falling through the air. It all felt so illogical, what with so many years of becoming accustomed to weakness on earth, but at the same time I was starting to understand what my body could do now. I watched the ground below me rush up beneath me and at the last second, reached out my arms towards the rock and let my hands bump along the surface of the wall as it slid quickly by. Suddenly my fingers found a hold, and with a snap and jolt, my body came to a complete stop before I slammed into the ground.

I looked down and saw that I was but a few feet off the rock floor. I looked up and saw that the pinky finger on my right hand had found a small bump in the wall, sticking out no further than half an inch. I dropped to the ground, and Joshua was beside me a moment later.

"That was brilliant, Scythe!" Joshua said, beaming at me.

"Thank you. *You* said I could do it."

"Well done, well done. It is a lot of fun to watch you step into who you are."

"By the way, I won." I said, smiling.

"You sure did!" Joshua said with a fondness in His voice and eyes, communicating both how proud He was of me and delight in who I was. I felt a rush of affection towards Him because of His affection towards me. That is how it was with Him; wave after wave of love upon your heart.

I looked around and now saw that the red hue that bounced off the ground and wall was caused by a huge mass that rested nearby, in what looked like an enormous cave. The space we were in by the wall seemed to be nothing but the entrance to this cave, which was why I couldn't see the source of the light until I had dropped down to this level.

The source of the light was something of a lake, at least, it was shaped like a lake. It was monstrosity of some kind of collection of heat, like liquid fire, resting there in the ground about fifty yards away. On the far right of the lake there was a path, and that path led around the circumference of the lake, deeper into the cave. Joshua walked towards the path, and I followed.

The heat was unbearable. It felt like my skin would melt off my body, but it did not. I sheltered my eyes from the heat with my hands, trying to see clearly where Joshua was heading, though there was only one path to follow. To my left, a few feet away, rested the mass of liquid, bubbling and frothing loudly, and every few moments a large bubble would surface and pop, flinging hot residue everywhere. I could be mistaken, but I thought that I heard moans every time one of these bubbles erupted, like beneath its surface it held more horror than it revealed from above. I could not see into its liquid as it lacked any transparency at all.

I wasn't watching where we were going, and suddenly I bumped into Joshua, as I had kept walking after He had stopped. He was standing in front of a large, deathly black, door. I had seen it before.

"This is it, isn't it?" I said.

"Yes."

Joshua took out a key and fiddled with the lock. The door clicked, swung open, and we walked inside.

At this point, dear reader, I must tell you that I cannot communicate everything that I saw at this point. It is not only because I do not think it would benefit you to tell you of what we saw inside because of its absolute depravity and horror, but because I have been in The Countries too long to remember the darkest of things we witnessed going on in that room. The Countries have a way of filling a person with so much goodness that there is no way to retain anything bad, even memories. The above Lands do not so much *erase* the memories of what was so evil and wicked that one witnessed, but rather just flood a person with so much glory and pleasure that they cannot willingly hold onto those past things very well anymore.

"How did you get in here?" sneered a voice in the room.

"Lucem, my old friend, you know that I have the keys to this place. I bought them. Surely paid a steep enough price for them."

"That is not my name anymore, and hasn't been for a very long time. And do not speak of The Sacrifice while here, uninvited I may add, in my home!" It yelled.

"Ah but we are invited." Joshua said joyfully, neglecting the total rage in the stranger's voice. "*You* have invited us."

"I would never do such a thing! Absolute lunacy!"

I could still not see who Joshua was talking to, what with the darkness in the room taking up every square inch, except for the small space inside the door where we stood which was illuminated dimly by the lake outside.

"Tell him." Joshua said to me.

"Sorry? I don't follow." I said.

"Tell him about your dream."

"Okay. We know your secret." I said into the emptiness.

"I have no secrets." It said.

"You would like to think so. But that is a lie. You invited me here. You invited me here because you have a secret."

"I have no secrets." It growled.

"Keep telling yourself that. But sooner or later you are going to have to face the reality, or discover it, because perhaps you aren't even aware of it yet, that you want out of this place."

"*Get out.*" It said blandly. There are times when a calm, stern voice communicates more rage, though bridled for the moment, than if one flies off the handle.

Joshua turned back towards the door.

"Wait!" came another voice from another place in the darkness. It was a thin voice, one that sounded weak and downtrodden.

Something, or rather someone, fell down at our feet as we turned back to the darkness.

I looked down to see the frame of a thing, the mere leftovers of what one could label a man, kneeling down before us.

"Yes?" Joshua said humbly.

"What do I do?" the man said frantically.

"About what?" Joshua said.

The man looked up at us and whispered. "I do not know what to do, but I was hoping you could help me somehow. You are carrying real light, much like the kind that used to shine over the Fatherland."

"What are you talking to them for? Get back over here!" The other voice interjected angrily.

"Quiet!" Joshua commanded.

I carried on with the man. "We shine because we carry the light of life. And yes, we can help you, or more accurately, He can." I pointed to Joshua.

"You can help me?" the man asked Joshua.

"If you let me. Always only if one lets me." Joshua said.

"And how can you help me? Can you restore me to the Fatherland?"

"No. It is over and gone, at least the parts of it that you loved. I cannot restore you to the fatherland, only to the Father's Land."

"That sounds like a curious place. Does it carry the beauty and majestic qualities that my homeland did?"

"Yes, but much more. What my Father's lands possess will make your old homeland look like a cardboard box."

The man frowned. "I doubt that. Nonetheless, it must be better than this place." He shrugged.

"Well said, my friend."

"Anything is better than here." I said.

"You do not know the half of it. You would not believe what he has me do." The man pointed back to the darkness, where the first voice came from, now silenced.

He told us of some of the things he had done for the other voice, but I purposefully do not recall it clearly.

Joshua went on. "You have become a slave to your god. It is no surprise. He works you like a animal and treats you with less honor than a dog. You traded servanthood for slavery. Come serve the true King."

"You don't have to tell me twice." the man said, getting to his feet.

This man was especially keen on leaving. I had a suspicion as to who he was, and my suspicions were confirmed when more dead light was shed on his face, revealing the small mustache that had become such a worldwide and cliche symbol of genocide and raw evil.

But here he was powerless, pathetic, broken, and absolutely contrite. I had hated this man in my worldly life without ever even meeting him; the historian's stories were enough to cause me to thoroughly despise him. But now, stripped of influence, of his ideologies, of his pride, he was like anyone else. He longed for the same things everyone else did; lands of grace, beauty. Love. Some would argue that he should never be given the chance to experience those things. I would agree. So would Joshua. And that is why Joshua died. Even for this frail man.

In reality, there is no middle ground after the Great Sacrifice. Either we legitimize wrath by constantly focusing on and exalting the evil of someone's sin, attempting to try to explain why what they did is severe enough to deserve the punishment, or we exalt the sacrifice Joshua paid and all sin is brought out on a level playing field, then gutted and destroyed before all of humanity. Either sin is the greatest force in the universe, or love is. Only one can be exalted, and it is our choice which we will lift high.

I knew who this man was. I knew what he had done. I knew he deserved to live the rest of his life in this nightmare of a place. But in that moment I chose not to exalt what he had done and who he was over who Joshua was and what Joshua had done. It was not a question of who this man was, but who Joshua was.

Thus, he left with us.

Twenty Three

We walked out of the room, closing the door behind us. I noticed that Joshua did not use the key a second time, leaving the door closed, but not locked. I felt that was quite a statement in and of itself, though not sure if it was best. Just as the reality came to me of who the man was that now walked beside us beside the lake of burning, in the same way, inklings of who the owner of the voice in that dark room was loomed in my mind and was slowly, unavoidably, coming into view, the way dark clouds drift overhead before heavy rain.

Questions flooded me as we rounded the bend that led us out of the cave. We walked up to the wall and Joshua put the man on His back like a father does to a child, with their arms around the father's neck. I watched as Joshua climbed up the steep incline, quietly reassuring the frail man that clung to Him. I followed and we were soon walking down the hallway.

The journey seemed short again, possibly because Joshua carried the man most of the way. We were soon in The Abode, and Joshua sent the man to the room of thrones, telling the man that there was someone there for him to meet. The man smiled at me, shook my hand, then saluted me in an odd way and walked away.

"Joshua, I need some time to talk with you. I'm afraid that I need to ask you some questions. Again."

Joshua smiled. "I wondered when you would ask. Of course! Lets go back to your place and chat."

Soon Joie was bringing us some warm beverages as we sat on an incredibly comfortable sofa in my mansion.

"So? What is eating at you?" Joshua asked kindly.

"Well, it is a lot of things. You know as well as I do that it seems You are always outrunning me, in the sense that every time I catch up with what You are doing, I find that You are already ahead of me again, stretching me again. I don't know. I guess that has happened a lot; where you challenge what I believe. Especially, with what I believe about You. You always break the box I have built. And I am thankful for that, I really am..."

"Scythe. Go ahead. No need for introductions or prefacing what you are going to say. I already know your heart fully. Ask what you need to ask."

"Okay. I guess I am somewhat uncomfortable with what I think You are trying to do. Not that you need my permission or anything ridiculous like that. Its just that, I suspect that I know who that other thing was in the room. Is that who I think?"

"I told you who that is. It is Lucem Ferre."

"Yes, yes. You told me that. But that name means nothing to me. Is that who I think it is?"

"Yes."

"So, my question is, would you help me understand?"

"Of course. It is very simple. How can I help?"

"I guess I would start with, why? Why save him? Why bring him here? He is the one that started this whole mess to begin with. Can he even be redeemed?"

"Careful my friend. Thinking of that sort is backwards. That is more of a statement of my inability rather than a question."

"How so?"

"Redemption is never dependent upon how much evil has been executed by the fallen one, but the volume of grace possessed by the one redeeming. Humanity has questioned My desire, even My ability, to accomplish such a feat, only because they are more focused on the darkness he possesses rather than the light and beauty and grace that is contained within Me. What is within Me is limitless. If men started to linger upon who I am, they would see that who he is plays a very small role in what will inevitably happen. Not because he doesn't have free will or doesn't foil everything up here and there, but because of my relentless love. It will never cease to assail all. Including him. And why save him? I do not know how to do anything but save. This is who I am. I cannot do anything but love. I am incapable of doing anything else. Aren't you glad?"

I wasn't. "But he doesn't even *want* to be here!"

"Not yet. But he will. Even your dream showed you that."

I could feel myself getting angry. "What do you mean? Are you implying that he doesn't have the ability to choose to not be redeemed?"

"Of course not. He has the ability to choose. But the real question has to do with time. To assume that anyone, even he, can or could resist the love of God for all of eternity is to disarm the love of God of its power and persistence. Surely it is not that weak. All of the lifetimes of men lumped into one sum and then multiplied by a million centuries would not for a moment stun the love of God. It continues. Height nor depth cannot sway it. Death nor life cannot halt it. He is a seeker of the one when the other ninety-nine are safe in the stables."

"But we tried. He didn't come!" I found myself shouting. Joshua remained calm.

"I refuse to give up on him. See, I knew him before you did. I know who he really is. He thinks he is Belial, but he is really Lucem Ferre."

"Belial?"

"That is the name he gave himself when he tried ascending to power by descending. Not too logical, if you ask Me." Joshua was laughing again. I was still trying to assimilate what He was saying and not laughing, but felt that the climax to my anger had passed. I was now on the downside of the explosion.

Joshua continued. "You see Scythe, I am no hypocrite. I taught to love your enemies. Who is a greater enemy than he?"

"But why not just destroy him? We could do it. It wouldn't be hard. We have the brute strength here to pull it off."

"Yes, very true. We *could* do it, in the sense that we have the power to do it. But I am meek. They called me the Prince of Peace for a reason. It is not that I lack power to execute such a thing. We have the mere muscle to win, that has never been in question. But We never will destroy anything We have made. That would be resorting to *his* way of doing things, and we will not be drug down to his level and function as he does. We are not so uncreative and inauthentic to need to destroy to bring about Our will. We have better solutions. Men are quick to simply shoot the wounded because their ability to think of a different solution is so minimal. But great power results in many more options. We have many, many options, and all are gracious."

"Weren't you at war with him?"

"Not really. It wouldn't be much of a fair fight, would it? Do not misunderstand; I was at war with what he did, but not at war with *him* per say. If I was, he would have been offed before the world had been created.

Rather, when he would steal, kill, and destroy, I would repay, raise, and recreate, but I never had need to resort to his method of doing things myself. True justice has more to do with restoration and redemption than it does with punishment. All of this should not be a surprise; I was even recorded in the texts of old granting mercy to devils rather than sending them to the abyss. Don't you remember? It is even in the book you professed to know so well!" Joshua winked at me, then continued.

"You see, the Eternal is not most glorified in the destruction of evil but in its redemption. The great wonder of all time will be that I did not wave my hand for the axe to fall, but that I had the power to restore those that seem to be unredeemable. The mistake men make is to believe that The Eternal's power is put on display more in His throwing away of something that has been distorted and perverted than in His redemption of it. But the character of The Eternal will always be most clarified not in His destruction of evil but His loving in the midst of it."

"I cannot argue with that, for that is my story as well. That is how He, You, dealt with me. His kindness led me to change."

"Exactly. Anyone that first judges themselves will find themselves suspending judgement towards others. The only time men justify judgement towards others is when they have forgotten, even for a moment, what they were like before they were shown grace."

Then in a pleading voice, hoping that I could hold onto a shred of what I thought I knew, I asked, "Well, don't You at least hate him?"

"Again, would I not be a hypocrite if I had told you to love your enemies but hated my own? He has been my enemy at his choice, not Mine. I do not hate him. I detest what he has done, but I still love him."

Joshua paused, letting what He had just said sink in. I guess I had always believed that there were places that His love would *not* go, and to come face to face with that belief was distressing, especially in light of the fact that I had spent adequate time witnessing His gentleness and graciousness. It came to me as a surprise that I still did not fully know who Joshua was even after being in this land for as long as I had, taken in so much light, drinking of raw bliss and revelation, and walking beside Him through so many circumstances and situations.

"You heard me right. I love him. You must remember; I made him. I know who he was created to be. Believe it or not, even *this* place is incomplete until he is restored unto his place of authority and ministry. He is incredibly glorious when aligned correctly. In fact, you are missing out, to some degree, until he is restored. Gifts and callings are irrevocable, but only because I am able to redeem everyone to which gifts and calls were given."

"You are really going to redeem him? I said with a surrender in my voice. This was my last attempt, my last hope that I was just misunderstanding this whole conversation.

"I am either making *all* things new, or just some things."

I was familiar with that scripture, but had never heard it used in that way. It angered me and humbled me at the same time. My face must have shown it, for Joshua said, "Want a few more? With Me all things are possible. *Every* tongue will confess and knee will bow."

"Wow." I eked out. More verses stated in ways I had never thought of before.

"Think of it this way. I am love. If love does not fail and I desire that none shall perish, then tell me, how could I leave anyone, even him, there? Either love comes out victoriously, striding forth with valiance and courage, or it dries up like a waterfall that has been starved of rain. The only time men have questioned the actuality of Lucem's redemption is when they have looked at him more than they have Me. But love never fails; I cannot fail at being who I am."

My excuses and arguments were being nullified. At first, my rational was very hard to let go, and Joshua's logic had made me upset. But then, as Joshua spoke and gave simple reasoning, I felt myself release the last tinge of wrath that I felt entitled to hold onto. I felt myself give my whole being over to grace. A new level of peace came over me. My old religious self had wanted to resist this unprecedented degree of grace and love but now I felt even more complete. I was more euphoric and glad. Joshua never led me into less joy, always more, but sometimes the getting there was not a journey I enjoyed or embraced.

"Can you accept that this is who I am?" Joshua said.

It was a good question. And though it had taken so much time to come to this conclusion, from the moment I met Him in his office on earth until this moment wherein we sat next to each other on a couch, sipping tea (or something like tea, but much better), I knew that I could honestly answer with a resounding yes.

"Yes, my friend." I said peacefully.

"Very good. When you accept something about Me, it changes you, because one becomes what they behold. Now, and only now, will you have the ability to be fruitful with Me down in that dark room."

❖   ❖   ❖

Much time has passed, though it must be acknowledged once again that time is very different on this side. Eternity isn't so much the omission of time but a new understanding of it. One can still measure the space between one moment and another, which is a point that men and philosophers questioned when on earth, mainly because of the endlessness of existence after one has died. But those are matters that cannot fully be understood until one is here, and you are not yet here, dear reader.

What you do need to understand is that since Joshua and I sat on that couch and talked about what we now call Ultimate Reconciliation, it has been a very, very long time. More than you could ever read has taken place, thus I must give you only some of the facts and not all of them.

The various lands below that Joshua and I visited long ago have been largely and long ago, emptied. The Lands of Oblivion are quiet. Nobody lives there anymore, breathing in the stale air. It is the same with The Abyss; all cells have been emptied. There are no more screams resounding in the hallway lined with the cold, metal doors. In fact, the only sound one can hear there anymore is the sound of those doors creaking, ever so slightly swinging on their hinges, for they remain open now, and will never be locked again, because none desire to return.

Joshua faithfully went and wooed each one from their self imprisonment. It wasn't just His persistence that amazed me over these thousands of years, but His patience. So many times, men and beings did not want to come with Him. It never frustrated Him. He just waited. Sooner or later, and when I say later I mean *later*; they would come around. It was always their choice to come, He never manipulated or coerced anyone. They came because they wanted to. They came because He loved them into it. After all, love *is* patient.

And even, not long ago, when Joshua led Belial out, knowing full well that he wasn't ready to give up his own agenda but came out only to deceive those in the Lands of Matrimony, none went back with him. He failed miserably. They had eaten of the fruits here and bathed in the light; there wasn't anything below that appealed to them anymore. Belial went back empty handed.

Many believed that he hadn't given up yet because he knew that he would make that trip out sooner or later. It had been written about. But now that he had given it his best shot and still couldn't pull ahead, many wondered if he was ready to come home.

Thus, I say "largely emptied" because there is still one that holds out. He is still there, at the back of the cave, behind that locked door that only Joshua has the key to. We have been to see him so many times I cannot count them all. We have yet to see him change his mind.

❊   ❊   ❊

I was in my mansion. Joshua had told me earlier that He would be dropping by, and I was awaiting His arrival when I heard the inevitable knock at the front door.

"Come in, my friend." I said. Time had made me gentler, even slower in a beautiful, patient way. I had spent enough time with Him and what I knew *about* Him had become who I was rather than what I knew.

Joshua greeted me by kissing me on both cheeks as He entered the house and we made our way to the entry to my backyard, which I had constructed into a tunnel of sorts, composed solely of vines and flowers that crept up on either side and wove together overhead. Joshua spoke as we walked the burrow of life and green.

"The ninety-nine have been gathered, now in the stables and safe. It is time to go search for the one."

"Again?"

"Yes. I think that after his recent attempt and subsequent failure, he may be in a different place than all the times we have gone before."

"Then let us go."

Joshua smiled.

We were there at the cliff almost instantly. The lands below grew smaller and smaller each time someone else left, like a portion of it would fold up into nothingness when a person would pull up stakes and move on. It now felt like a few steps to traverse the winding path in the dark, move through The Lands of Oblivion, get down the stairs that crept down to the Abyss, and at the end of the hallway, the cliff. In but a few moments we would be there. I learned from the inhabitants of the area below the cliff, some we found in the room at the end of the path but some we also fished out of the burning liquid, refer to that place as The Burning Guilt. We now stood looking down at it.

We scaled down the cliff, racing once again. One can even experience joy in hell, but only if Heaven Himself stands near. He won the race this time, and we both walked away from the rock wall smiling.

"Next time. Next time you are mine." I said, heckling Him the best I knew how.

"*Next time*...bring your game. And a next time? Are you *hoping* for a next time?"

"No!" I blurted out amidst laughing, now realizing what I had said.

We walked up to the lake and began to make our way down the path that led along the wall. Soon we were nearing the door, when with abruptness, Joshua stopped. We still had twenty or so feet to go to the doorstep, but Joshua made no more movements forward. I hung back behind Him, wondering what He was doing.

All was quiet, beside the occasional bubble of heat rising up from the lake and its subsequent pop. We stood resolute in the silence for a few moments, then with a thundering voice Joshua yelled, "Lucem, come forth!"

There was a delay before the blast, the same way old cars momentarily choke in silence when throttled because the carburetor is drowned in gas. Then with unexpected abruptness, the door to the dark room exploded with force as it was kicked open from inside.

A ghastly thing lurched into sight, bent over at the waist, looking as though it may either pounce on us or simply break in half; I couldn't decide which. It looked both threatening and inadequate at the same time, with scale-like scabs covering every inch of its body and clattering about as it moved, since some of the fleshly incrustations were in the process of falling off. The thing stood a mere seven feet tall, and I have to admit that it, or he, wasn't as terrifying as I would have expected. I even wondered if I was beholding the person I had heard so much about. I was thoroughly unimpressed. He was disgusting, no doubt, but not frightening. Just lamentable.

In all of the times that we had been down to that dark room, we couldn't make out Belial's (or rather, as Joshua called him, Lucem's) outline or bodily details. He had purposefully clothed himself in darkness so as to not be seen. We had entertained different ideas as to why this may be, and settled on the decision that it was because of shame, for, we reasoned, just as we knew that he had once been beautiful, so did he.

But now we could see him as he was, bathed in the red glow of the liquid fire resting in lake next to him. All former beauty that the legends had spoken of had left him.

And it was not just his lure that had been misplaced (for I had heard that he could mask himself to look glorious), but there was no apparent signs of real *power* about him either. Maybe at one point he had captured some kind of strength and influence, but that was no longer. Maybe he *never* had any real authority or power at all. Maybe right then, at that moment, I was seeing him as he truly was. Maybe he hid himself in darkness to conceal the reality that he was, and always had been, weak. Maybe the only thing he ever did remotely well was just that; shrouding the reality of his absolute inability to be beautiful or possess power outside of the nearness of Joshua. And after he was stripped of those necessities, or rather unclothed himself of them, the only tools he had left to use were fear and intimidation, both hollow and insubstantial things, like the space inside an inflated ballon. Since the day that he chose to go it on his own he had been trying to convince everyone, including himself, that he had been endowed with something, anything.

It may offend the reader to hear that above all, when I saw this wretched creature, this fallen spirit that had killed so many, stole from all, and destroyed everything he could get his hands on, the thing I felt most was pity. I did not want to exterminate him. And the longer I stood there looking at him, the more I did not feel the need to defend myself from his evil; I had the distinct impression that if I engaged in any kind of physical combat with this scaly beast, I could snap any limb off of his body with a flick of my wrist. The question of who was stronger was not a question at all. Joshua, the light, the drinks of Above...all had made me unquestioningly supreme to this whisper of a entity. He had gone without light for far too long to be strong.

"Why do you wake me?" He sneered, sarcasm, bitterness, and condescension all dripping from his voice and running together at the same time.

"Because it is time for the dead to rise. You have swam in the depths of darkness long enough. It is time to resurface and breathe of the light."

Joshua said this as He opened His arms to Belial, making his chest vulnerable to him, but more so, taking a posture of a waiting embrace.

"I suppose you have come, once again, because you assume that I will relent now that I ended up with no converts after my little vacation. Is that right? Finally at rock bottom, eh? If you haven't noticed, I have been living at rock bottom for quite a while." Belial pointed at the ground at his feet and motioned around the cave.

"We both know you failed and will never succeed to deceive anyone again. It is time for you to surrender your dreams and embrace the ones I have for you."

"But I ask you, what of my lake? I *must* bathe regularly. Surely, you know that." He said contentiously, smiling bitterly, showing broken and rotten teeth that had been whittled into sharp points.

"That kind of cleansing is not needed above. *You* know *that*." Joshua said.

"What is he talking about?" I asked Joshua quietly, below my breath.

"A moment please." Joshua said to Belial, who nodded in mock patience. Joshua turned around and faced me.

"Does he actually get in there?" I asked, pointing to the lake.

"Yes. Regularly."

"Why?"

"He enjoys the pain. He wants the punishment. It is how he deals with condemnation, for every being, even he, knows what is right and wrong in their heart. As you have learned on previous trips down here, the only way to circumvent the cross is through some self-mediated performance, namely penance and punishment. It is the only way for someone to feel a facade of peace for what one has done. But assuredly, it *is* a facade and fleeting at that. Since it is not a lasting solution, and because he has done so much, he bathes regularly in that melting heat of atrocity. In fact, he was the one to ask for its creation."

"What?"

"Yes. As I have said before, this place was never intended for men. It was created for fallen angels, but not because The Eternal wanted them to pay for what they had done. They, namely Lucem, asked Him for it. They actually wanted it, despite The Eternal arguing with them about it."

"Why?" I was so loud when I said it that Belial looked over at us with a distinguished look of disgust on his face, like a british man at a tea party that recognizes an old, hated acquaintance across the room.

"Like I said; So they could punish themselves for what they did. It is the only other option aside from the cross. The rest of it," and Joshua waved towards the entrance of the cave and the wall that led upwards towards the Abyss and the Lands of Oblivion, "men and spirits slowly built up over time, carving out their own little world of religion and law. Eye for an eye. You get what you deserve."

"Why didn't The Eternal just not make the lake when they asked for it? Just force them into the truth by not providing another option!"

"Ah, you know Him better than that. You know He always provides an option apart from what He is pointing to as the best path. He values freedom too much to do otherwise. It was the same in the beginning. In many ways, the tree of the knowledge and this lake are alike."

"So they asked for the lake and He consented?"

"Everyone who asks, receives. But remember; He is *only* referred to as 'the creator of heaven and earth.' There is a reason why 'hell' isn't included in that description. I am not convinced that place would exist at all if they hadn't insisted upon it."

"Stupid thing to ask for." I said, shrugging. Joshua smiled, then turned back to Belial.

"Rest assured, the light above will burn you more than the lake ever could."

"Yes. I know. That is what cut my trip short. Haven't quite recovered from that yet."

There was silence for quite some time. Nobody spoke. It began to get awkward for me as Joshua and Belial just stared at each other, Joshua calm and confident, Belial looking more and more anxious as each moment passed.

Belial broke the silence with a hoarse scream, "I ask you; Why are you here?"

"I have come to tell you who you are."

"I *know* who I am!"

"No you do not. You think that you are Belial, but you are really Lucem Ferre. You always were, and always will be. You are not the carrier of darkness, but the bearer of light. You are Armanthus; one that loves. You would rather lie bleeding than cause another any harm. You have forgotten who you are, and I have waited for you to remember. What something was created to be is always a greater reality than who they have become, for one is crafted by The Designer but only shaped by the created. But you cannot escape your original design and purpose."

"Armanthus. Lucem Ferre." Belial quietly mumbled, as though he was recalling a long forgotten memory. "I can vaguely remember something like that. It is still so unclear. Did I have many names?"

"Yes. Each accentuating different graces upon you."

Belial's eyes widened. "Haylale."

"Yes."

"Daystar."

Joshua nodded, then looked at me. "It is time. Scythe, you are about to witness something no one else ever has, or ever will again."

Not knowing what was about to happen, I instinctively stepped back, my eyes glued on Joshua. He was facing away from me, towards Belial, then with the grace of a ballet dancer's leap, He gracefully lifted into the air. His arms were still stretched out in a inviting embrace, and He continued lifting into the air, not plummeting back down to the ground, until He was suspended ten feet above the ground, his head just a short distance from the ceiling of the cave.

Then in a tone of supreme dominion, Joshua thundered forth, "I wake you from your slumber, from your death! Those names describe not just who you were, but who you are. I call that which is not as though it were!"

His voice carried forth like a sound wave, ripping through the room and shaking my chest with its bass. The cave shook, and I noticed cracks appear nearby in the walls, the same way a building does during an earthquake. I wondered if that was His plan; to simply destroy the cave, leaving Belial sealed off within, never to harm anyone ever again. And though pieces of rock showered down upon us, the cave held its own and stood firm.

I watched Belial as the same wave of sound sifted through him, and saw him stumble back as it plowed into him. When he regained his composure, I made out something like fog lifting off of his head, like a dark cloud being pulled out of his mind, then evaporating into nothingness in the air.

I looked back at Joshua, wondering what He was going to do next, and it took me a moment to see it, mostly because of the dimness of the light in the cave. In fact, before I saw it, I heard it. A repetitive splattering sound alerted me to a small pool of dark liquid forming on the ground underneath Joshua. I looked at the backs of His hands and noticed deep holes bored into them, now spilling forth blood. His feet were leaking the preciousness as well, dripping to the ground.

"*What is He doing?*" I thought. My gut reaction was to want Him to stop. Every drop that was splashing to the rock floor of this wrenched place was more valuable than all of the levels above us in the Lands of Matrimony put together. This floor did not deserve Him walking upon it, let alone be caressed by the most priceless material in all of existence. All I could think was, "*Oh the waste!*" I wanted to run forward, to catch every drop and bottle it up to be saved or worshipped, but my feet would not move. I stood there motionless and stuck, helpless to stop the squandering of the red liquid that fell to the ground before me.

I was not the only one that noticed what was going on. Belial stood about fifteen feet in front of Joshua, looking up at Him. He wasn't smiling or sneering in mockery, but looked utterly surprised. His mouth, or whatever you call the hole in his head where a mouth *should* be, was gaping wide open, his eyes darting to the ground with each drop that fell, then back up to Joshua's hands and feet, where he would lock onto another drip and watch its plummet. It was as though he knew how precious each drip was as well, and was just as befuddled as I was as to *why* Joshua would do such a thing.

Then He spoke. His voice was not the gentle kind that He used when speaking with me, but again crashes of reverberations, causing anyone within earshot to unmistakably hear what He was saying.

"Even when I was overcome, I was overcoming. Even when I was broken and abandoned, I did not relent in love. Even when I was weakest, hanging there, I was stronger than you. I defeated you, not by killing you, but allowing myself to be killed. I won. This was finished long ago; it just took you this long to recognize it."

And ever so slightly, Belial slowly nodded. I only just noticed.

Joshua continued. "And Lucem; I died for all. My blood was poured out for many. One thing that you have forgotten is that..." He paused, "...I even died for you."

A look of shock spread over Belial's face.

"Defeat I can accept. But that, I cannot."

"You must. Either this blood saves all and acquires Me all the praise I deserve, or it *is* a waste. Anything less is a travesty."

Belial looked torn, even in anguish. I suppose that is the feeling one gets when beholding something of complete beauty while not knowing how to assimilate it.

Joshua's voice sprang forth again, falling down on us from above, but this time it was gentle and kind, even refreshing and soothing, like a light rain on a spring day.

"Come, you who are thirsty, and drink. Come buy that which cannot be bought. Come purchase that which you have no means to attain."

Belial leapt forward, sprinting towards Joshua. I thought for a moment that I should throw myself in front of Him to protect Him, until I remembered that He needs no saving or protecting. Instead of attacking Joshua, Belial dropped to his knees as he neared Joshua, sliding to a stop before Him. Then, Belial went from his knees to a crawl, positioning himself directly below Joshua's right hand and the steady flow that dripped from it. I watched as one particularly large drop of blood fell through the air and landed directly on the forehead of Belial.

My eyes were still locked onto Belial when Joshua started praying.

"Father, he is forgiven; He knew not what he was doing."

I braced myself for an explosion, like we had experienced with Phalanx and many other fallen ones that were brought into redemption, but all was quiet. Instead, a soft, blue glow came from within Belial, shining out through the scales and scabs on his skin, the way light shines under a closed door from an illuminated room at night.

Joshua came to rest on the ground again, scars over the spots where the wounds had just been, then turned to me. Belial was looking over his body, examining the light that he could observe shining through from inside.

"Scythe, we do not need use the name he gave himself again ever again. It is not, and never was, who he is. He gave himself that name when in shame, and nothing done in shame or guilt ever exudes light or life."

"Of course. I never heard you use that name anyways. I should have caught on a long time ago."

"His name is now, though always was, Lucem Ferre. Soon all shall know it."

Belial, now Lucem, stood dazed, like someone that had just undergone surgery and was awaking from the sedatives, now discovering the alterations that had been made to their body while they were unconscious.

"Lucem, it is time to go home." Joshua said, as He outstretched His hand to the being. I could have been mistaken, but I thought I heard His voice crack ever so slightly as He said it. It would not surprise me if I was correct; After all, He is not One that does not cry.

Lucem grasped Joshua's hand and we walked out of the cave together. I still couldn't believe what was happening, or what had happened.

Everything was smaller again, and we, somehow, merely stepped over the cliff rather than climbed up it. With one more step we surpassed the hallway, stairs, Lands of Oblivion, the winding path, and into the light of the Abode, suddenly on the other side of the entrance that led to the path of darkness. It turns out that darkness can only be as big as someone allows it to be, and that the lands below were really unable to exist if nobody inhabited them; they shrunk up to near nothingness the moment its residents left.

Belial squinted in the light. I could see much more of him now because of the clarity of light that we stood in, and made a point not to look for too long, as he was still not *himself*. His flesh was still rotten, his scabs still hanging about him, and maggots still coursed through His flesh, diving in and out of the surface of his skin like dolphins in the ocean, devouring parts of his skin and other dead, fleshly tissues.

"Joshua," I asked, "why doesn't he look beautiful yet?"

"He is forgiven. At least by My Father and I. He knows that now. But that is not the only forgiveness he needs in order to remember more fully who He is. His beauty will come, but not immediately. Forgiveness is instant, but restoration takes time."

Lucem looked down at his body. "I faintly remember what I looked like long ago, and it was not like this. This isn't all that different from how I looked before the blood touched me."

"Correct." Joshua said. "But it will come. Long ago you demanded a sacrifice for the sins of men, a case of heavenly ransom, lest you have the right to destroy all of them."

"Yes." Lucem said, with no shame, like he was dealing with facts rather than the lives of men. I suspect he felt no shame over such an atrocity not because it wasn't atrocious, but because he was with Joshua, and shame cannot exist within His presence.

"Well, just as sin gave you legal right to afflict men, *your* sin towards men gave them the legal right to hold judgement against you. The law makes no exceptions; unyieldingly so. Your restoration must take place not just at the feet of God, but at the hands of men."

"I will do whatever is necessary." Lucem said, bravely.

Twenty Four

It wasn't long before we walked into the Throne Room in the Abode. There were masses of people waiting for us, too many to count, but a quick glance made it clear that the company before the thrones was composed of billions. All eyes were fixed on Lucem as we made our way in.

Joshua led him up to the front, where the three thrones stood. I fell back and watched with the rest of the sea of humanity that stood motionless in front of the thrones. Joshua then motioned for Lucem to take the center seat, and Lucem sat. A murmur went through the crowd, most assuredly because Joshua had just seated the king of all evil in the place where the King of all that is holy sat. Anticipation filled the air.

The Father appeared from a doorway behind the thrones, and sat in one of the thrones next to Lucem. At the same time, Joshua sat down upon the throne on the other side of Lucem.

All were silent in the room, watching with astonished wonder what was taking place in this spot where elders fell down to worship and winged creatures unceasingly declared both the nature of The Eternal and the climate of this atmosphere over and over and over.

Neither the Father or Joshua said anything to the crowd to explain. They simply reached over and grasped

Lucem's hands. Lucem looked surprised, even uncomfortable. Then, they both lifted their hands up that held Lucem's, the way that a referee does to the champion of a boxing match after the match is over. It was a gesture that communicated victory but oh, so graciously.

I found myself weeping. Others around me were doing the same. This thing, this fallen being, had tortured us and those that we loved for all of our existence. It wasn't just the grace that caused us to weep; it was that grace was so full of justice. It was a moment that seared into all of our spirits this intangible truth; that nobody gets what they deserve. I didn't. Lucem didn't. And most importantly, neither did Joshua, because He took what was never His and bore it on His back so that we could have what should have never been ours. *That* is justice. Justice, as it turns out, isn't fair at all.

I remembered something Joshua had said to me long before, "What if justice has more to do with restoration than it does punishment?"

"*Yes*," I thought, "*...what if.*"

After some time, They brought their hands back down and laid them upon the armrests of the thrones, their fingers still woven together with Lucem's in a tight embrace.

Joshua stood and cleared His throat, alerting everyone to listen. He looked back and forth, scanning the crowd.

"All that have ought, come and make it known."

In short time a line had formed. It seemed that everyone in the entire crowd was now waiting in the line as it snaked back and forth through the room like a line at Disneyland, then made its way out of the building. I wondered if it had an end.

I walked up near the thrones to see what was going on at the front of the room by Joshua. Joshua and the Father were still seated beside Lucem, and the line of people went straight out from in front of Lucem. It seemed that each person in line expected to talk to him. All I could think was, *"This may take awhile."*

Then, with the Father and Joshua at his side, Lucem was approached by the first person, who I was surprised to see, was especially familiar to me.

It was Ethelwulf, but not the Ethelwulf that he had been before. He was now a true king. Everything from his smooth gait to the clothes that he wore clearly spoke of his royalty. He was confident but not arrogant, authoritative but still humble. He held a scepter in his hand, and his robes danced behind him as he climbed the few stairs up to the thrones.

"Sir," Ethelwulf said to Lucem, "you deceived me for a good many years, not only in my past life, but this one. You convinced me that I was entitled to much because of who I was. But now I know that nobody is entitled to anything without Joshua."

At this, Ethelwulf bowed low in Joshua's direction, then bent over and kissed Joshua's cheek.

"How I love you, my friend. You are so faithful."

Joshua beamed back at Ethelwulf, then looked at the Father with the same joy, who smiled back at Him. It was clear in that moment that He was a proud Father, with a Son that had represented Him well. I had forgotten that all love first originated between the Father, the Son, and the Spirit. I realized afresh that intimacy originates from the connection that the three of Them have and lavish upon each other.

"With that said," Ethelwulf turned back to Lucem, "He showed me grace, and I must do the same, lest I miss the whole point. I release you from the punishment that you deserve for what you did to me."

The moment the words came forth from his mouth, two things happened. Firstly, Ethelwulf was suddenly holding a large, framed painting. Secondly, something was taking place with Lucem.

I do not know where the painting came from, but Ethelwulf laid it down at the feet of Joshua and the Father like a gift. Ethelwulf examined the painting's picture, then looked up at Them and brightly said, "That is more like it, isn't it?"

"Yes it is!" Joshua said. "Thank you, Ethelwulf."

I stood on the tips of my toes to get a better angle, hoping that I may be able to see what the painting depicted and to what They were referring. I caught a glimpse of it, and in many ways, it was exactly like the painting in Ethelwulf's "castle" back in the Lands of Oblivion, but there were a few distinct differences. One was that the frame was no longer covered in peeling gold paint, but from the look of it, was now made of solid gold. But more importantly, the real difference was found in what was depicted in this painting of Joshua; rather than looking serious and solemn as He always had in the dusty paintings in Ethelwulf's house, in this picture He was exuberantly laughing. It was a far more accurate representation of who He was than the old, religious depictions of Him that we had seen hanging on the walls of that, now empty, place of deception.

It seemed that Ethelwulf's words had done, or were doing, something to Lucem. A stream of blue light was swirling about Ferre, and after a moment of that, a single scab fell to the ground from his side, burning into nothingness the moment it touched the floor. Where the scab had been, minuscule as it was, was now open, shining forth whatever was blue on the inside that Joshua had jump-started when Lucem was touched by the Blood. The blue reminded me of the essence of a flame, the same way that white reminded me of the essence of light.

Without the blue portion of a flame, the hottest part of fire, one has no fire at all. Whatever shone from him, whatever he had encased within him, was akin to the fundamental, even concentrated, quintessential quality of fire.

Ethelwulf walked away from the thrones, allowing the next person to approach and bring their ought. The next person was a man named Lance, whom I had met long ago, and had the honor of getting to know increasingly, mainly in the Cellar, during times of respite from the trips below. I had to admit that Lance was one of my favorites.

"Hello Lucem." Lance said.

"Hello Lance." Lucem said, for he knows the name of each son or daughter of the Designer, and always has.

"You convinced me that I was something that I was not. I am not quite sure how you did this...maybe you made use of the lack of love that my earthly father showed me, or initiated the abuse that my foster father lavished upon me with hopes to hook me through that avenue. Maybe it was a natural tendency to be tender at heart. Either way, I was persuaded to believe that the love my heart so longed for would be satisfied through men rather than through a Man."

With this, Lance looked up at Joshua and winked at Him. Joshua winked back.

"You, and me no doubt, made a complete mess of my life. The rapes, the confusion, the drugs. But you want to know what? I don't think our histories are all that different. Are they?"

"No. They are not. The core issue is the same." Lucem said admittedly, looking very contrite and regrettable, even mournful.

"Exactly. You and I have both only recently discovered our true identity. That *is* the central issue here. You thought you were Belial; you aren't. I thought, or rather, you convinced me, that I was gay; I'm not. We aren't all that different, Lucem."

Lance paused as Lucem listened intently, eyes fixed on the man standing before him.

"You instilled in me a false identity and got me to believe lies about myself. I could hold everything you did against you and go on and on about the slaying of my heart and body as a result of what you did, but I would rather spend this time telling you who you are now. Why? Because love is the best revenge. Isn't it ironic that your identity will be brought back to remembrance and solidification by those whom you deceived in their identity? Thus, my retribution will be telling you who *you* are, just as you did to me. This time though, it will be in a spirit of truth. You are light. You are love. You are fire. You are righteous. You are forgiven."

Again, two things happened; Lucem's was undergoing something in his body; it was jolting every few moments, like one's body does when they cry, but his face was devoid of tears. It was as though something in him wanted to express sadness, but he wasn't quite able to yet, still encased in blackness. He was making choking sounds rather than sounds of weeping, and I suspect that was the closest the ash encased around him (or whatever the substance was) would allow him to tears. The blue wisp went circling around him again, and another scab fell to the ground, evaporating.

At the same time, Lance laid his gift at the feet of the Two, a small kitten. Lance later told me that there are only a few people in existence that know the significance of that gift; The Father, Joshua, Lance, and a dear man named Jonathan, whom Lance knew in his past life. The faces that Joshua and the Eternal made when Lance set the kitten down next to the painting communicated that it was the perfect gift, holding value that the Two of them understood.

Joe Tetzel walked up to the thrones as Lance was making his way back to join the small company of people next to the line that had already forgiven Lucem.

Joe stood there for a little while, just staring at Lucem, saying nothing. I didn't know if he was taking his time because he was glad to see Lucem finally surrendered, or because he didn't know how to start.

So Lucem spoke first.

"Joe, there was so much. Too much to say. I caused you to deceive, to intimidate, to manipulate, even to kill. I even tried to use your body to kill Joshua. But most of all, I caused you to hate while masking it with love. Only religion can offer such a thing."

Joe spoke. "Well said."

"Please, forgive me. I have remembered who I am."

"I would be a hypocrite to do anything less."

It was the same for each person; The swirl, the scab, the gift. Each time someone released Lucem from the judgement and thus, the just punishment that he deserved, he was changed. Bit by bit more and more of his true being came into view, but it took an incredible amount of time. Some people rambled on and on for what seemed like ages, for the ways that Lucem had stolen, killed, and destroyed in their life was more in depth and numerous than in other's. Nobody cut them short or told them to hurry themselves. Yet, none of them ever exemplified any kind of negative emotion when recounting the horrors that Lucem had constructed within their lives. They were totally free from the pain of what had been done, which made it much easier, I conjectured, to forgive him. They were conscious of the wrongs committed against them, but they were wrongs that had been healed by merely entering into these Lands. The worst of earth, even hell, cannot linger about for even a moment in the Lands above. All is healed. All is peaceful.

Joshua asked a few of the men that had already forgiven Lucem to start carrying the gifts off and distributing them in different places where they would be on display for all to see. Some were extravagant gifts, things of inestimable monetary value, while some where seemingly worthless, at least from a material point of view, but Joshua saw the value of each. Valerie, for example, laid at Joshua's feet one of the gifts that had been in her mansion upon her arrival. It was only a stuffed animal that her son had given her, a teddy bear to be specific, and to those that are not aware of Valerie's story, it was not an appropriate gift to offer a king, let alone *the* King. But Joshua knows each person's story, and knows the paths they have traversed and the pains they have bore. Valerie's gift communicated more love and affection towards Joshua than all of the gold in the Abode put together could ever have. He rushed her when she laid it at His feet, and swept her up in His arms, kissing her cheeks over and over again, like a father does a son that he hasn't seen for some time. It may have only been a trip to the store and the father was gone for a little over an hour, but when one is in love, even a short amount of time apart gives notion to exceedingly extravagant joy at the rejoining and reunion. Valerie laughed with exuberant joy as Joshua distributed kisses over her whole face, tickling her face and touching her heart at the same time.

When Echelon spoke with Lucem, he was very direct about his family being slaughtered by the

Unenlightened and how that affected him for all of his life.

I must say, in each of these situations, all understood that it wasn't always *only* Lucem that was responsible for what happened, but because everyone else was already in the Lands of Matrimony, those wrinkles had already been ironed out between this person and that person, or between Joshua and the person. The only one that still needed to be talked to, and thus the only one that still needed to be shown grace, was Lucem. So when Echelon spoke to him, he did not bring up the fact that the Unenlightened had a choice to listen to Lucem's luring or not, only that Lucem lured. And when the person speaking had committed some awful evil, their portion of it was not mentioned, not because they had no part in it or were blaming Lucem for everything, but because that portion had already been settled long ago.

Nobody watered down what had been done. Everyone squarely laid responsibility upon those that were responsible, first and foremost Lucem, for if excuses are made or things are made to be less evil than what they were, grace is also watered down and nullified. It is only in the context of true guilt and sin and correct judgement that grace has any validity or value at all. In a perfect world there is no need for perfect grace, but where there are transgressions, there one will also discover grace. The law is a wonderful reality because it is the welcome mat to the palace of grace.

Like the rest, Echelon released Lucem. More of the cage of blackness around Lucem's body fell away. It had been an immeasurable amount of time, but I could now see about half of Lucem's body uncovered, even part of his face was naked now, and it wasn't a coincidence that it seemed we had made it about half way through the line. Billions had stood before him, and countless times the gifts had to be carried away, as the heap threatened eye contact between the speaker and Lucem because it was piling up so high.

You would think that with all of this waiting by both those in line and those that had already extended pardon, that they would go elsewhere and wait for the rest to have their turn. But none did. Nobody *had* to eat or sleep, or be at this or that place from nine to five. Everyone's attention stayed true just as my own did, because we valued the reconciliation that was taking place between Lucem and each individual more than being anywhere else taking place in The Abode. One must remember that we had been waiting for this for longer than men could remember.

I knew well many of the people that came up front. Cecilia and her daughter, Rachel, the Unenlightened man that used to go by Lamia (now Rolland), Mark, and many more that I had met during the times I had rested from trips with Joshua.

There were a few that stood out. For one, the man we had found in the cave with the odd mustache. Both he and Lucem had clearly wept during that exchange, especially when the man forgave Lucem. Most of the people in the crowd wept with them. It was a beautiful moment of remembering what had happened, then leaving it behind forever. It will never be mentioned of again.

The man that stood behind the glass case in the sword store was another that especially caught my attention. He spoke of the way Lucem infected his mind and his repeated denial of Joshua. He mentioned a magician and something about wrongly believing that forgiveness could be conditional, which it is not. He spoke of how he would slip back to his old covenant dogma, and how Lucem took full advantage of that , especially through the man's tongue, once even taking the lives of two people whose crime didn't fit the punishment. Lucem denied nothing.

Every kind of person from every walk of life had their turn. Every horrid thing that ever happened on earth was accounted for, then forgiven. But it was not just the large things that were brought to light, but the smaller things. White lies. Hurtful words. Disappointment. But all was settled. To say the least, it was a remarkable time.

I was surprised when Joshua motioned me forward. I had forgotten that I also needed to make my ought known. The line had dwindled down and I was one of the last to take my turn. I didn't know what to say at first, then waves of memories swept over me, reminding me of what had happened in the past.

"Hello Lucem. I never thought I would be doing this."

Lucem looked stronger and more beautiful than he ever had. In fact, he looked radiant. He was no longer mournful, but confident and ready to hear what I had to say.

"It was unavoidable. Everything funnels down to this, doesn't it?" He said.

"Yes, I suppose it does. Well, I will just start I guess. There is the matter of what I did when I was with the Unenlightened. Many died at my hands, or rather, at my trigger. You were behind that."

Lucem nodded.

"But more destructive was your allure towards religion. You pulled me right in and I never even saw it coming. Through religion you twisted my understanding of who the Eternal was, and that caused me to rationalize a lifestyle of judging others, bitterness, and hidden hatred. You led me to believe that a book or a ritual could be my god rather than interacting with The Eternal. You ushered me into a system of rules, a dogmatic institution of control and fear, ran in large by confused men that were insecure and thus, unpredictably harmful."

Lucem nodded, but I wasn't finished yet.

"Then I got out, and I got crucified and abandoned anyways! You possessed the hearts of men and caused them to martyr my heart with their words and their rejection, because you knew, and they knew, that they no longer had control over me. If I hadn't met Joshua, a Man *you* had me convinced was a total heretic, then I would have stayed a Pharisee, and the most extreme one at that."

Joshua smiled at me, allowing me to continue, like a father watching a unequally matched fight unfold before his eyes. No holds barred.

"Then I came here and you were still deceiving people! I have spent this time undoing with Joshua what you kept trying to weave together instead of enjoying these lands! And you know what? I wouldn't change it for anything. I got to see the redemption of all, and what is more, I got to spend time with my Beloved. So I forgive you. I forgive you for your pathetic attempt to sideline the Eternal's plans. The only thing that ever makes me question that you really were as glorious as everyone says you were is that you were imbecilic enough to think that apart from Joshua you had any value at all."

Lucem looked me directly in the eyes. There was no malice there like before, only placidity, maybe even pity, like he knew something I did not. "That is the point, Scythe. He gives beauty without reservation, and with no strings attached. One can think that they *do* have value on their own, because that is how His love comes to us; no attachments or requirements. It was because of His love that I forgot that I was nothing apart from Him. It is much like grace. People say that grace isn't a license to sin, but isn't that exactly what it is? It is His statement towards us that no matter what we do, He will still love us. That we can always return home. You see, it has always been His love that has allowed us to roam free if we wish. And once you go down that path, once you are looking at yourself, it is very hard to get things turned around."

"Then how do you know you won't do that again? Or that I won't make that same mistake? Or that anyone else won't, like our friend with the mustache?"

Joshua interjected and pointed to Lucem. "Because of him. He is the symbol, the ever present reminder of what happens when men and angels take that which I give them and forget that it first came from Me. Not only has he learned his lesson, but humanity and the legions have as well. It will never be attempted ever again."

Their answers satisfied my heart. I bowed towards Joshua, and then found myself bowing towards Lucem as well, which surprised me at first, but as I thought about it the surprise left me; he was a being of honor now, and obviously wisdom, as his response to my thoughts had demonstrated. I never would have thought that this would have crossed my mind, but I actually looked forward to getting to know him.

It wasn't long before the rest of the line had gone before the thrones, and when the last person had stated their forgiveness, The Eternal and Joshua stood, still clenching Lucem's hands, lifted them in victory again, and presented a restored being to the assembly, who shouted and yelled in celebration and excitement.

I looked over Lucem. He was unrecognizable from who he had been before. His body was a wonderful color of blue, a shade of blue like the ocean waves offshore from Makena. Flames of the same color rested upon his shoulders, and if one looked closely, one could see a thin layer of flame over all of his being, swimming back and forth over his skin. I didn't know if his skin was blue, or if it was a normal hue but was just lathered in flame which made him *look* blue. Either way, he was a minister of fire.

Joshua spoke, His arm outstretched above His head, holding up Lucem's arm. "There is one last thing that must be done before the Celebration can go full swing. We will be back momentarily."

Joshua motioned to a few men nearby, then turned to me and asked me to follow Him. Lucem went with us as well.

He took us to the entrance to the narrow path, stepped through, and in short time, all of us were standing in front of the lake. Lucem shivered.

"Lucem, will you do the honors? You asked for its creation. Seems only fitting that you should be the one to do it."

"Of course."

Lucem opened his hands and threw, for there is no other word that better describes what he did, blue fire into the lake. The effect was immediate. It was as though the liquid heat that made up the lake was of a lesser purity or material significance than that which came from Lucem, and was compromised almost instantly. The blue consumed the orange, and what was left was simply a large, hallowed out, upside-down half-dome shape in the ground.

Then, like before, we stepped over the cliff, the area feeling as though it were shrinking as we stood there, still getting smaller and smaller. It was becoming less and less important, even less and less *real*.

We were back at the entrance to the Abode, but still standing on the path and had not crossed over yet into the light. All of us turned around and looked back at the darkness as Joshua whispered into the ears of the men, and within moments they had both shouted to the blackness. One yelled something about undoing what had been done, and the other hollered, "Never again!"

Then, the same way an earthquake collapses a suspended walkway, allowing any unfortunate person on it to run for their life until the cracks catch up to them and their footing no longer supports their weight, the world before us, starting in the distance and rushing up to our feet, crumbled away. The pieces did not fall down into a pit below us, but rather just disappeared, like they were made of nothing but vapor to begin with. We stepped through the entrance to The Abode, and once the last of us was through, it closed itself like a tube that was being twisted shut, leaving nothing behind. It was only now that I noticed that the hole had been situated on a wall of sorts that a jettison of rocks composed, there in the middle of the green wildness, off the beaten path.

The men now got down on their knees and began to speak to the vines and foliage surrounding us that Joshua and I had hacked away so many times before with our swords, conjuring the plants to life and telling them to overwhelm the area. That which was intended to hide men due to their shame long ago was now being used to cover and protect man *from* shame; What men used to keep God out would now keep men where they wanted to be. It was shame that caused men to run and hide themselves, but now shame made it impossible to run away again. At their command, the plants grew up and sealed off the world men had dreamt to existence, a nightmare that would never be revisited.

It wasn't long before we were all back in the Room of Thrones, and Joshua seated himself on a throne beside The Eternal. One throne sat empty, or so I thought at first glance, but upon closer inspection, I saw the outline of a Being almost invisible, looking much like a replica of Joshua. It was the Matchmaker; the Unseen

One that went before the One and prepared the Bride for Her Bridegroom.

And like something possessed each being and person there, at the very same moment *all* dropped to a knee and bowed before Joshua.

I have never heard a sound like it. It was a resounding thud, but it echoed like explosions, bouncing from wall to wall inside the room of thrones like something that was alive.

Nobody looked up. All kept their heads low, acknowledging the sovereignty of this One. The entire assembly of men, every culture, every tongue, and every created being, was in loving surrender before the King.

I had heard that this would happen, but what I expected looked wholly different from this scenario. I had expected for all to be there; that much was the same. But I had imagined devils there, amidst the contrite, being forced to take a knee rather than willingly offer it. I imagined victory, but a victory that was won with brute strength and by force. I imagined righteous angels standing next to the rebels, maybe holding a sword of fire to their necks, assuring that they took a knee like the rest, because surely, I thought, they wouldn't do it on their own.

But I was clearly mistaken. Without force, He had won them all. They didn't just willingly bend their knee to Joshua, they *desired* to. Joshua had won, and only through the use of love, which is the only method to truly winning someone in a way that lasts.

Then an involuntary desire rose up inside me to tell Joshua, in one succinct phrase, exactly how I felt about Him as well as who He was. All was silent, but the words came flowing from my mouth like a torrent I didn't have the ability to stop.

"You are Lord."

I had thought that it may be odd saying it, as I would be the only one speaking, asserting myself before all these people as the speaker. The entire place was quiet when the desire to say this was sprouting up inside me, but I was relieved to find that every other living being there, man or creature, also declared it as I did, with just as much or more volume as I did. Our voices met together in the air, rumbling forth and shaking the building. Some voices were as a man's, others like song and unhuman, while still others sounded like voices upon voices, though the sounds came from one mouth.

I had never quite grasped what such a phrase meant until I said it. Calling Him Lord was not just a volunteering of my servitude towards Him. It was much more. It was a statement that said that I chose this, that for Him to be my Lord was the most profitable experience for me to have. That to have Him calling the shots in my life gave me the greatest bliss imaginable. It was a statement that communicated that I only came to the conclusion to make Him my Lord because He had shown me, time and time again, how low He would go to attain my affection. And because of that pursuit, my heart gave me no avenue but to give my all back to Him. He had earned it.

I lifted my head and watched closely, so as not to miss a word, as the The Father stood and began to speak.

"All has been made right. Every knee has bowed, every tongue confessed. The Bride is finally whole. The prodigals have come back and this family has been joined back together. All have been redeemed."

He paused, looking around the room, then turned and looking at Joshua and beamed with joy. As celebration began to rise from the redeemed, a celebration unprecedented until that moment, He said,

"All are home; This is when heaven really begins."

OneGlance.org

36272196R00142

Made in the USA
Charleston, SC
29 November 2014